'Ten of the Best'

Val Baker Addicott

Copyright © 2015 Val Baker Addicott
All rights reserved.
ISBN: - 10: 1511426349
ISBN-13: 978-1511426343

DEDICATION

To all my readers who have encouraged me to keep on writing.

CONTENTS

Page 1	Henry & I
Page 27	Love is the Sweetest Thing
Page 61	When you Wish Upon a Star
Page 95	Merlin
Page 143	Heaven on Earth
Page 149	My Guardian Angel
Page 159	Tea for Two
Page 169	The House on the Hill
Page 193	This Little Pig Didn't go to Market
Page 205	Like a Phoenix Rising from The Ashes.

ACKNOWLEDGMENTS

To Eryl Lynne for taking the front cover picture and David Redd for his advice and encouragement.

HENRY & I

I feel guilty sitting here writing this as I am breaking so many vows that I have adhered to for a lifetime. I only hope and pray that the Lord will guide my hand as I write these words. My days are numbered; I am well passed the three score years and ten that was prophesized in the Holy Book. Am I being vain in wanting to let people know that if only my life had been different I could have changed the course of history? Perhaps, when this manuscript is complete I will put it in a casket and bury it deep in Mother Earth and long after my bones have turned to dust someone will find and read my words and it will be up to them if they reveal what might have been and the hardships I have endured to keep this secret.

My childhood was idyllic spent in Greenwich Palace; my mother was so beautiful and brought many a look of admiration from the handsome knights that attended the King's Court but there was only one love for her, my handsome father who held a high position as one of the gentlemen of the Privy Chamber. As, at that time I was the only girl I was dressed in fine silks and luxurious velvets. Until my birth and later those of my siblings my mother had held a position of lady-in-waiting. The Palace was my playground and as I grew older I joined other children at their games. By the time I was eight year old my constant companion was Henry. I do not quite recall what began this friendship; perhaps it was because we both celebrated our birthday on 28th June; Henry being one year older as he was born in 1491. I took it as a compliment when he said 'I was better than any boy'. When I asked him why his brother Arthur didn't join us at our games he told me that it was because his brother would one day be King and he had to receive daily tutoring in the laws of the land and of the Catholic Church and learn Latin, French and Spanish. 'I am The Duke of York', he would remind me 'and you must obey my every wish'. He taught me to shoot an arrow and to catch fish and to ride a horse. What would my mother say if she saw me sitting astride across the pony's back; ladies only rode 'side-saddle'. He also passed on the knowledge of languages and reading and writing that he had learnt in the palace classroom. No-one took any notice of us as we chased each other through the long golden corn or swam in the river; Henry, more often or not, as naked as the day he was born and I in my drawers. We were children, innocent and naïve of what went on behind the closed doors of the beautiful Palace at Greenwich.

All that was to change when in the year 1501 Arthur married Catherine of Aragon. I remember the event as if it was yesterday it was the time when everything between Henry and I changed. We had arranged to go horse-riding and I enjoyed the thrill of trying to out-ride Henry. We tethered the horses to a low lying branch. The November day was cold and bleak but Henry put a rug around my shoulders; 'perhaps this should be our wedding day' he remarked as he pulled me close and began to kiss me. He began to fumble with the buttons on my riding habit.

'Stop it Henry this isn't fun I don't like this game.'

'Remember what I once told you that as I am a Royal Prince you must always obey me. I want to find out what it is like being with a woman. You are not that naïve; you have seen what the courtiers get up to in the corridors of the palace.'

'One thing I do know is that I am not a woman; I am just a child. Sorry Henry you'll have to wait a while before I'll be interested in fornicating with you.'

'I thought you were my friend; I couldn't help but notice when in the summer we swam together your breasts were already sprouting hopefully by the spring you'll be ready for breaking-in and I want to be the first. Perhaps I had better find a wanton trollop to teach me 'what's what'.

'Ask your brother he's the married one'.

'Doubt if he knows where to start; poor Catherine perhaps I should break her in for him. He's too weak to mount a horse let alone a woman.'

I remember laughing at the thought of him breaking-in any woman.

'What do you find so funny?'

'You; remember Henry I too have seen you naked and at the moment you haven't got much between your legs; I doubt if any woman would enjoy your fumbling.'

My words must have really riled him as he left me sitting by the river and rode off in the direction of the Palace.

Three weeks elapsed before I saw him again; this time it was a totally different situation. He sent his messenger to ask me to meet him in our usual meeting place. The day was clear and frosty so I wrapped up warm with many layers under my fur coat; smiling to myself that no way would he be able to molest me beneath all these layers.

I was surprised to see him running towards me and taking me in his arms he began to sob bitterly. I kissed him on the cheek; a loving, sisterly kiss. 'What troubles you?' I asked.

'Haven't you heard Arthur is dead and before his body is cold there is rumour rife in the court that the King wishes me to marry Catherine to keep the peace with Spain?'

'Don't be silly Henry you can't marry your brother's widow the pope would have something to say about that.'

'They say he never managed to break her in. He never had an erection or he didn't know what to do with it. Now if you let me show you how I can please you and then I will tell my father and he will insist I marry you.'

'I keep telling you Henry I am not yet a woman; I doubt if making love to me will bring you any pleasure.'

'We could try; come to my rooms and I will make you feel like a Princess.'

'The time isn't right; you had better go back and comfort your mother. When I am old enough I promise I will be yours.'

There were so many changes during the next years; firstly, I became a woman and my parents began planning who would make a suitable husband for me. All I could think of was Henry did he really mean that if I let him make love to me he would tell his father he wanted to marry me. I felt sick at the thought of the suitors my parents were suggesting; to me they all were at least twenty years older than myself; some already having a paunch from drinking too much ale; being in court I also knew that some already had more than one mistress and illegitimate children. Henry had always told me that I was pretty so why should I have to marry one of these obnoxious men?

Dispensation had been granted by the Pope so now a treaty had been set up that Henry; now with the title Prince of Wales and Duke of Cornwall should marry his brother's widow but at that time Henry couldn't cohabit with Catherine as the Court ruled he was too young. Gone was my chance of marrying Henry and one day becoming Queen.

After Arthur's death I saw very little of Henry as his father appeared to keep him out of the prying eyes of the courtiers. No longer did I run freely in the meadows and woodlands; instead I sat with the other ladies embroidering or been taught music all so boring to me. When I saw the ladies busy about their tasks I would creep silently from the room and make my way to the library where I would find a cleric at his desk. So much I learnt from these religious men; the love of books and how to put words on parchment. My parents had always said there was no point teaching a girl to read so I never disclosed my knowledge to them. Obviously, I was unaware, at that time, what an advantage this would one day be.

The year was 1509 I was betrothed to a widower more than thirty years my senior; a wealthy landowner. We had met just once and at that time he had treated me as if I was a filly up for sale in a farmer's market. He had questioned my mother with regards that I was still a virgin as he didn't want spoilt goods; he had pulled up my skirts and rubbed his huge rough hands over my legs; as it was a warm spring day I had on a fine cotton shift. He roughly grabbed at my young breasts and began to fondle them.

'Enough,' my father said; 'she is not yours yet.'

'I'll be down south again in November; arrange a wedding for the second Monday in the month.'

All I could think of was how could I get a message to Henry but on second thoughts I realized it would do no good as he was betrothed to Catherine. Mad ideas kept creeping through my mind; surely if Henry 'broke me in' that horrible old man wouldn't want me but there again what of the large dowry father had paid this man?

My plans were shattered as on 21st April 1509 old King Henry V11 died and my Henry became King Henry V111 what surprised me more was that it was by his declaration that on 3rd June 1509 he married Catherine of Aragon in Greyfriar's Church; quite a low key affair for a royal wedding; prior to their Coronation on 23rd June.

The Coronation was a huge lavish celebration that went on for days. Celebrations began on 21st June when Henry rode from Greenwich to the Tower of London. On the eve of the Coronation Henry and his new bride led a procession to Westminster. The pageantry was magnificent with the Knights of the Bath dressed in splendid blue gowns and the King wore a robe of crimson velvet trimmed with ermine; a jacket of gold decorated with diamonds, rubies, emeralds, pearls and other precious stones. The route they travelled was also decorated with cloth-of-gold and tapestries. Even Henry's horse was dressed in ermine and cloth-of-gold and the canopy held over him by the four barons was also the same. Then came the master of the horse followed by the Queen reclining in a litter covered by an ornate canopy. On her long auburn hair she wore a bejeweled coronet.

It was a time of great rejoicing; a time that the people felt would put an end to ancient hatreds and reunite England with Spain. There was a feeling of magic in the air and I must admit I was hypnotized by the feeling of excitement. I, with my mother, had a fine position in the Abbey as father was involved in the ceremonials. As I saw them walking under canopies carried by the barons I closed my eyes for a fleeting moment as I saw a vision of myself with Henry; as he walked by did I catch his eye as on that occasion I felt as beautiful as any Princess, My dress was a vibrant green velvet and for the first time mother had insisted I was now old enough to wear a tightly laced basque that enhanced my young well-developed bosom. As soon as the King's procession passed the carpet was torn to shreds by the excited crowds who wanted souvenirs of this memorable day.

The Archbishop of Canterbury presented Henry to his people who called out 'vivat, vivat rex' 'Long Live the King'. Tears swelled in my eyes as the Archbishop anointed Henry with Holy oils; gone was my childhood friend no longer would we run through the cornfield or ride bare-back along the river-side he was now my liege. All the important guests returned to Westminster Hall to a lavish banquet that was opened with a fanfare of trumpets and a special procession of dishes, led by the Duke of Buckingham and the Lord Steward on horseback. The celebrations didn't end there as there was a special tournament that night and then two days of jousting and feasting; it was the end of an era and the beginning of a new age. I had hoped that I would become one of the new Queen's Lady-in-Waiting but they had been dashed when I had become betrothed and I now knew that I would, after my wedding, be taken to live in the north of England.

My mind was in a turmoil; between drinking too much and dancing and frolicking my head was spinning and my heart racing with excitement. I needed to escape; I wanted to find a room where I could take off my shoes and rest for just a while. I ventured down a candle-lit corridor passing a few couples in what my mother would have referred to as 'a compromising situation'; at the end of the corridor I noticed a door that was ajar and as there was no-one about so I entered. A small candle cast shadows on the ceiling and from the flickering light I noticed the walls were lined with books. Feeling confident that no-one would leave the banquet to come to this room I sat down on a velvet settle and slipping my feet out of my slippers I lay back upon the cushion. A breeze encircled the room cooling my dizzy head; I closed my eyes as every bone in my body began to relax. I was just about to drift off to sleep when something disturbed me; the creaking of the door and another brighter light. It was Henry carrying a lighted torch that he placed in a holder in the wall.

'I've been watching you all evening; you looked so enticing like a woodland sprite'.

'You followed me?'

'It is so long since I have seen my little play-mate I thought it was time we had some fun. Do you remember my little temptress that you once promised I would be the first and now you have broken that promise by getting yourself betrothed? Was the old codger any good in bed?'

'I haven't given myself to him so I wouldn't know; he wants me to come to him as a pure, innocent virgin.'

'My luck is in then.' Henry sat down beside me and began rubbing his hands over my tender feet.

'That's feels so good,' I said laughing as he tickled my feet. It didn't stop there his hands began to move up my legs as he lifted my dress.

'I always knew you were a free spirit but to come to a banquet without your bloomers is asking for trouble; but so much better for me.'

I tried to pass off his comment by saying that I wasn't used to wearing such a heavy dress and I felt I would be too hot. I then asked him wouldn't the Queen be missing him?

'She has retired; it has all been too much for her as she is with child.'

'Shouldn't you be with her?'

'She doesn't allow me in her bed-chamber now I have filled her belly. Have to look for companionship where I can get it and you my little princess I know will not say 'no' to you King.'

I was betrothed and it was a condition of my betrothal that I was a virgin I couldn't let Henry take me here. I went to get up but Henry pushed me back.

'Not so fast; I want what you promised me; it can be here on the settle; against the wall like those in the corridor or on the table but I am going to break my filly in.'

He was a big man and would easily over-power me it was not worth trying to escape him. His hungry lips bruised my tender mouth; he undid the front of my dress and began to fondle my breasts with his large rough hands and then fully aroused he entered me. I screamed; I felt no pleasure as he was not gentle with me. Satisfied he moved off me and crossed to a cabinet where he took a bottle of wine and two glasses.

'I don't want any more wine I am going back to the banquet.'

'You are not going anywhere until your King has finished with you. Drink this and make your King a happy man.'

I drank the wine and a second glass and once again my head started throbbing and I began to feel inebriated.

'Come dance for me like you danced in the hall; lift up your dress and entice your King.'

I remained seated.

'Dance I said; dance, I order you to dance.'

There was nothing I could do but obey him; I twirled around to the sound of the distant music; lifting my skirt as he had ordered me to do. Suddenly he grabbed me and raising my skirt he pulled me down onto his lap. For a fleeting moment I was unaware of what was about to happen until I felt him hard against me.

When he had fulfilled himself he roughly pushed me to the floor; 'that was good my little sprite I know where to come looking when I need some comfort.' He left the room laughing.

I never saw Henry again.

It was the middle of July and I couldn't understand why I hadn't had a bleed and each morning until about mid-day I felt so sick. I began to think that I was ill and that I was dying. I had been to confession but hadn't confessed to the priest that I had sinned as it would involve Henry and no-one would believe me but the previous Sunday I had told him that I had evil thoughts and believed that I was dying because I was feeling so sick. What one confesses to the priest was for his ears only but to my horror he must have told my parents.

My mother summoned me to her room; 'Have you been lying with a man?'

'No mother.' How could I tell her that Henry had taken me at the banquet?

'You are lying to be you dirty trollop. Who is he? How can you now marry we promised you as a virgin and now you are with child. I was ashamed to see how you flaunted yourself at the coronation banquet; my daughter showing her legs to all and sundry. You must have shown more than your legs to some man. Who is he? He will have to marry you.'

'He is already married.'

I felt my mother's hand hard across my face,
'My sister will sort you out you brazen hussy.'

Suddenly I was afraid; her sister, my aunt, was a nun from a convent in France who had been spending time with us as she had been visiting Canterbury.

'Sorted out', I most certainly was before the week was over my aunt and I left England for France; never again did my feet tread on English soil.

Although it was summer the crossing was rough as a terrible storm raged in the channel. My aunt spent the time on her knees praying and told me to do the same as it was because of my sin God had sent the storm.

At that time I wasn't that concerned about being taken to the convent as I was aware that my father had given my aunt a fine gift of money for the Abbey but I couldn't understand why he had given her my jewels and none of my finery was sent with me; I only hoped that she had my jewels for safe keeping until the time came for me to leave. How naïve I was. We disembarked at Calais and that night we were given a room at a nearby convent. All I wanted to do was sleep but at intervals through the night my aunt woke me and ordered me to kneel in prayer with her; the time was about two o'clock, I felt that I had hardly been asleep when again she woke me; daylight was just breaking in the east. She ordered me to wash and be ready for breakfast. The mention of breakfast made me realize how hungry I was but the thought of food made me feel sick. I needn't have worried because there was no sign of the lavish breakfast I had anticipated. I lay back down on the makeshift bed and watched as she ate the bread and drank the ale.

'I will go to my devotions you may rest until I return from Prime and then we will travel on; we should make the Abbey before nightfall.'

We travelled on foot for what seemed miles; I was so weary and not only was I feeling sick but now it was combined with pangs of hunger. How I wish I had eaten the bread at breakfast. If I hadn't felt so poorly I would have found the scenery so beautiful; the golden corn dotted with the red of poppies and the peasants working happily in the fields. It would be a hard winter for them if the storm we faced in the channel found its way across to France the downpour would ruin the crops. A mile or so further I managed to have a ride on the back of a wagon and the farmer told me to help myself to the fruit from the baskets he was taking to market. Although I rode my aunt still insisted on walking and at intervals stopped at the way-side and knelt in prayer and then opening her bible began to read passages from the scriptures. Since leaving the convent in Calais she hadn't spoken a word to me it was if she had suddenly taken a vow of silence.

The farmer dropped us at the market that was a hive of activity how I would have loved to have seen more but yet again my aunt took me to another convent where she appeared to be well-known. I was left to my own devices as she was ushered to the noon prayer of Sext None. I found myself in the kitchen and the lay people working there gave me freshly baked bread and a large bowl of vegetable broth. I returned to the main hall and found her dining in an anti-room. The nuns dined in silence whilst one of them read from the bible. After the meal she said her 'Good-byes' and we travelled on. As we were about to enter a dense wood the sun suddenly disappeared behind a black cloud and the heavens opened. We were soon drenched to the skin but my aunt in her thick black cassock fared better than myself in my thin cotton shift that clung to every curve of my body and no longer could the soft mound of my belly be camouflaged. Oak, ash, elm, sycamore all reached for the sky and formed a canopy above us, although dense, it still gave us very little cover. I was near to tears and my feet were swollen and bleeding and I began to stumble over every pebble and tree root; falling to the ground and getting covered in mud. How cruel I felt she was as she took no heed to my plight. I had no idea of the time as the wood was so dark but judging by the time we had stopped at the last convent I guessed it must be about five o'clock. To my amazement she suddenly stopped and kneeling by the side of the woodland path began her ritual of prayer. I was later to learn the prayers at this time was Vespers after which the nuns would have a light supper. Drenched to the skin in the middle of a wood she took from what appeared a deep pocket a loaf of bread, now sodden with water and breaking it in half passed me a piece. There was nothing else for me to do but eat the pulp. By the time we left the wood the rain had eased and a watery sun appeared in the heavens and after passing through a few villages we began a climb up the mountainside; as the sun began to sink in the west I noticed a magnificent building encircled by the sunlight. This was not our place of rest as it was the Abbey. We saw no-one it was as if the place was abandoned but as we began to descend the hillside I noticed the lay-folk still working in the fields and below I could see the walled confines of the convent. Lay-folk; 'servants' far out-numbered the religious inhabitants. At wealthy Abbeys the ratio was thirty workers to every monk. These workers baked bread and brewed ale; laundered clothes and served the meals and also cared for the horses.

I felt a sudden relief; I would be given warm water to wash the grime from my body and clean clothes and a warm bed. It was not to be; I was ushered by a young postulant to what was nothing more than a cell. It contained a wooden 'cot' on which was a thin straw mattress and a coarse blanket. A cross was pinned on the wall above a small table on which stood a jug and basin.

'Where is my aunt? I wish to speak with my aunt. Surely I am a guest here.'

She mumbled to be in French that my aunt had gone to Compline the last service of the day and from there she would retire to bed.

How disillusioned I was; I thought I would be a 'guest' at the convent but as I just mentioned I found myself in the cell; obviously unaware that it was to be my abode for many years to come. I wasn't invited to dine with the nuns and my meagre allowance of food was brought to be by the same novice I had met on my first evening. Each night I cried myself to sleep and word of this must have got back to my aunt as by the end of the week a nun came and lectured me about my sins and saying that I had too much time on my hands and instructed me to go to the kitchen and get water and get down on my knees and wash the corridor. My job never ended as there seemed so many corridors to scrub and as the weeks went by and my belly grew large with my child I found the task so tedious. My knees hurt and my hands were raw; still I cried at night but now I made sure that no-one heard me. As the time came near to be delivered I felt a little more relaxed as surely when baby arrived I would be free to leave.

It was blowing a gale on that March day when I went into labour; for the first time since my arrival the nuns who attended me were kinder. I was taken to the room where they treated the lay folk of the village; from what I had seen of the convent a far more pleasant room. As I was led into the room I noticed a man and woman sitting in the corridor; why had my eyes fixed upon them? The reason being that they didn't look like peasants as they were lavishly dressed. I soon forgot about them as my pains got beyond my limit of endurance. I screamed as yet another pain gripped me but was told by one of the nuns there was no need to make such a noise and another said I was letting the devil out. Then I heard my baby cry and one of the nuns placed my son in my arms and immediately his little rose-bud mouth grasped at my full breast.

'Henri' I said; 'I shall name him Henri.'

I observed two nuns deep in debate; it was as if the one who had given me my baby was having a lecture from a more senior nun. I listened to their conversation as Henri happily sucked at my nipple.

'You shouldn't have given the baby to her.'

'But she is the mother; it is her child.'

'She was not to see the child we were supposed to take it from her and say that it had died. His new parents are waiting in the corridor.'

When I heard these words I started to cry; 'He is mine; he is my son my Henri.'

My baby was snatched from my breast and wrapped in a blanket and in a hysterical state I shouted; 'His name is Henri. I want my son; my Henri.' I was silenced by a hard slap across my face.

'There is no place here for a baby we have received a large donation for the Abbey.'

'He is my son,' I wept; 'I will be leaving now and I will return home with him to England.'

The younger of the two nuns took my hand; 'What made you think you are returning home? This now is your home you are to remain with us and soon you will become a postulant and then after five years a novice and then within two years you will become one of us. You will long for your wedding day when you will dress in white and we will celebrate the day you become a bride of Christ.' The nuns made the sign of the cross and bowed their heads. The combined shock of child-birth; the loss of my baby and the fact that I was never to leave the convent hurt me more than the slap I had received from the nun. I fell into a silent stupor. I just did as I was bidden; one of the nuns bound up my breasts to stop the flow of milk. I was given a clean shift and with the aid of the nicest of the nuns was taken back to my cell. There was no spirit left in me; I tried to call to my baby as I saw him in the arms of the woman as she left the confines of the convent but nothing left my lips.

Each day; each week; each year were all the same to me. The seasons were the only thing that brought change to my monotonous life. Eight years had somehow disappeared unawares to me. I was now a fully-fledged nun; a bride of Christ. Events that happened in the Convent such as my aunt dying and also the Mother Superior brought changes to my life; I was now a well-respected member of our close community and also classed as a learned one. I spent long hours copying manuscripts and also travelling, all be it on foot, to distant convents. Our convent was quite 'well-off' as we had many paying guests who gave us money to find a safe haven with us for whatever the reason.

Over the years the visitors brought news of the happenings in the English Court. I had learned that Catherine's baby born on 10th January 1510 was stillborn and then a year later a son Henry was born but only lived seven weeks. If only things had been different my healthy son could have one day been king of England. Then in 1516 a daughter Mary was born.

It was after one of my visits to Calais when I saw him; as far as I was concerned I could not be wrong. He was taller than the youths he was with but it was not just that which made him stand out but also his shock of red hair; I knew at the very moment I set eyes on him it was my Henri.

'Henri,' shouted one of the lads; 'offer the nun some fruit'.

I sat myself down on the bank under the shade of a tree and thanked him for the delicious ripe berries. Soon the lads all gathered around me asking me questions about my journey and had I seen any large sailing ships in the port. One of them said that he wanted to be a sailor; another was going to join the musketeers. Then Henri spoke.

'My parents have promised me to the monastery; a vow they made the day I was born.'

'They will never take you,' laughed one of his friends, 'you are lazy with your lessons especially with Latin.'

What made me say it? The words were already out of my mouth. 'Ask your parents to get in touch with the Convent and ask for Sister Magdalena; if the Mother Superior agrees I will visit your home once a week and tutor you in Latin.'

I spent many hours at prayer and did penance for my sins but yet deep down I could not cast aside my longing to be close to my son if just for a short while. At his adoptive parents request I journeyed once a week to their magnificent chateau on the edge of the village. They treated me with reverence and showed no sign that they had any knowledge that I was Henri's mother. The young girl who had given birth to their adoptive son was English by now I was as French as anyone born in the country. I continued to tutor Henri for two years; he took an interest in his lessons and I suppose I can say a bond developed between Henri and myself. Obviously, I knew when Henri would reach his 12th birthday but there was no joy in my heart that day as already Henri had reached the age when he was to go and live at the Abbey and be tutored by the monks.

In 1519 a traveller brought us news from England that Henry's mistress Elizabeth Blount had given birth to a son who had been named Henry and the King had given him the title of the Duke of Richmond. How could I not show my feelings? Doing penance would not take the thoughts from my mind and my heart. One bastard was a Duke and mine was a lowly monk. Hearing this news seemed to bring to light again the time when Henry planted his seed within me.

As the years went by I constantly awaited to hear news from England. In 1525 I learned that Henry was tiring of Catherine as he so longed for a son and heir. Rumours of his affairs multiplied and also that he now wanted to marry one of the Boleyn sisters and because the Pope wouldn't give him dispensation he announced himself the head of the Church and broke all ties with the Pope; we heard tales of terror as Abbeys and Priories were raised to the ground. Then in 1533 we heard that he had married Anne Boleyn; rumour was told that she wouldn't become his mistress and because his longing was so great for her and her beauty he rid himself of the Catholic Church in order to make her his wife.

September brought us news that a daughter Elizabeth had been born at the Palace of Greenwich. Memories, memories of our halcyon days at Greenwich. He had found love and had his children around him; why had I to suffer a life of poverty for loving Henry?

This love wasn't to last long as in May 1536 she lost her head at the Tower of London. I prayed for him to be forgiven; surely, the Henry I had loved, was not capable of such a deed. I prayed for the soul of Anne and for the motherless child Elizabeth.

Over the years I learned of his marriages and even more beheadings. I settled contentedly into convent life and now prayed to be forgiven for my sins and put Henry from my mind. I saw my son on a few occasions when visiting the Abbey. I hoped that my tuition had borne fruit and helped him to rise to the position of Abbot; I suppose his adoptive parent's wealth also helped.

In 1547 I heard that the King of England had died aged fifty five. Henry's beloved wife Jane Seymour's sickly son Edward, aged nine, became king; he died in 1553. It was a turbulent time in Britain; Lady Jane Grey became queen for only nine days and was beheaded by Mary, Catherine of Aragon's daughter who became queen and endeavoured to bring Britain back to the catholic faith. After a fake pregnancy Britain lost faith in Mary and after her death Elizabeth was brought to court and was crowned Queen in 1558. The name that is on everyone's lips is Good Queen Bess.

I have now reached the promised life-span; three score years and ten. Who would have thought back in 1510 that I would out-live my son? I have finished my writings and today when I pay homage to our Abbot I hope I will be able to take from my robes this little box with my rolled and sealed manuscript and secretly place it in the folds of his shroud.

As each nail was knocked into his coffin it was like a dagger stabbing at my heart. If only things had been different I would have so loved my Henri. To have been able to watch him play in the long grass at Greenwich just as his father and
I had done. I close my eyes and pray that perhaps, one day, a monk or a farmer will find my son's remains and this little box and the contents will reveal who he really was; the son of Henry and I.

The End

Val Baker Addicott

Love is the Sweetest Thing

I sat in the corner of the ballroom feeling really out of place why had I been persuaded to come to the New Year party? I still had my coat on, not just because I felt cold but because my only decent dress was creased and there was a stain on the front, As soon as I had stepped inside the door with my friend from the store I knew that it had been a big mistake. Pat had said that it would cheer me up and help me to 'forget myself'. Instead it had done the opposite. I could feel the tears welling up in my eyes as I listened to dance music; 'Love is the sweetest thing-----'. It had been my mum and dad's favourite song. I really had to get out of the room; no-one would miss me as they were all having a fantastic time. I could but not help noticing a man sitting across the room as he was very conspicuous as he still wore his trilby hat that was pulled down low on his brow. He looked really sinister as he had the appearance of what I imagined a gangster looked like from movies I had seen. I got to my feet just at that moment when everyone started cheering and counting down the seconds; ten, nine, eight, seven, six, five, four, three, two, one. Happy New Year. I was jostled from side to side as everyone began toasting the New Year, Someone placed a drink in my hand and kissed me on the cheek; 'Happy New Year babe wanna dance?' I was quite close to the door a few more steps and I could make my escape. I closed my eyes and took a deep breath ready to push my way through the throng that had gathered at the entrance. Then I felt a strong hand on my arm, I opened my eyes and gazed into the face of 'the gangster' my heart missed a beat because the face of the man hiding beneath that hat was so handsome but his eyes looked like a stray dog that had been ill-treated and then I saw the scar.

'Happy New Year'. He kissed me on the cheek.

'Happy New Year,' had the words really left my lips. 'I have to leave.' I began to push my way through towards the door it almost felt like an impossible task as more and more revelers were joining the party.

As soon as I got outside the chill of the cold night air hit me; it wasn't just cold it was freezing. Perhaps I should have stayed at the party as at least it was warm in the room as now I was shivering. I only lived a short distance away but what had I to go home for? In the distance I could see groups of people all celebrating the new year; they had a lot to celebrate after six years of war the country was at peace and it was only right to bring in the New Year of 1946. I crossed the bridge making my way home; with every step I felt more and more down-cast. I stopped and leaned over the bridge and watched the dark depths of the river below. No-one would miss me; no-one would notice me as everyone was having a good time.

'Perhaps you would like me to see you home?'

It was 'the gangster' and by the light of the wintry moon he could well have been Humphry Bogart. I just nodded my head feeling guilty of the thoughts that I had just had. My teeth were chattering and I was shaking from head to toe. He put his arm around me and suddenly I felt safe. We walked on in silence and within ten minutes reached my basement flat.

'Thank you', I said as trembling I put the key in the lock. 'Would you like a coffee?' Why had I asked him in? My flat was nothing but a hovel; just one bare room and a small galley kitchen.

'Thank you, we need something to warm us up. I just want to make sure that you are okay. By the way I am William, what shall I call you?'

'Natasha; Natasha Kirov.' I lit a candle that stood on a small table by the door; it was the only light I had as I had no money for the meter. He sat down on the sofa unawares in the dim light that the springs were poking through. I went to the kitchen and put the kettle on the gas ring and scraping the bottom of the tin of condensed milk I spooned the contents into a mug; one of the war-time issues with no handle, luckily there was just enough camp coffee. Just as the water was beginning to warm the gas spluttered and went out.

'Hope it's okay' I said as I placed it on the table.

'Aren't you having one?'

I was near to tears; I was cold, tired and very depressed. How could I tell him that I had no money for the gas or the electric and worse still for food? I had eaten the last of a loaf of bread the morning before.

'Here, put this around you,' he said picking up a grubby rug from the sofa. 'Shall I put the gas fire on?'

'There's no gas,' I began to sob. 'There's no anything.'

'Where's your meter?' I pointed to the cupboard. I heard the coin drop in the meter and light flickered and cast a shadow making the dismal room look even worse. Then I felt the heat from the small gas fire as the one bar turned red.

'Come drink this coffee you need it more than I do. How come you are living like this?'

The tears that I had been holding back flooded from my eyes. 'I don't want it I feel ill.'

He put his arms around me and held me close; I could feel the warmth penetrating from his body. I felt like a child again being comforted by my father when I had fallen down but this wasn't my father this was a stranger. Gradually my sobs subsided and although the coffee was barely warm it tasted good.

'Are you going to tell me why you are living like this?' He led me to the sofa.

'Watch where you sit, the springs are sticking up. It all started when my mother and father were killed when a bomb dropped on our home. We had all been so happy; Father had left Russia in 1917 and met my mum at her parent's newsagents in a small village outside Oxford; they were married and moved to London and I was born in 1925. When the tragedy happened I was in secretarial college and dad was a hairdresser in a gents' outfitters and he had also become an air-raid warden. I was at a friend's birthday party the evening of the air-raid. We had all gone to the air-raid shelter and when the 'all-clear' sounded I made my way home only to find I had no home and was told both my parents had been killed. I stayed at my friend's home for a few weeks until I had finished college but her parents decided to leave London and go and live in the country with her grandparents. So once again I was homeless. Luckily I managed to get a job in the gent's outfitters where my father had worked and was able to rent this flat.'

'Didn't you have any relations that you could have lived with?'

'No-one; my grand-parents had both died and my mother had no siblings.'

'How come you ended up in this situation?'

'At the end of the war when the men returned home it was a case of last in first out as they made room for the men looking for employment. They had served their country so they had a right to have their old jobs back. I lost my job in October and have managed to keep going until now but I haven't paid the rent since before Christmas and the landlord wants me out but I keep avoiding him as I have no-where to go.' Thoughts of everything began filling my head; it was all making me feel ill I couldn't keep talking. I just wanted to close my eyes and never wake up again. I felt as if I was drifting away; I could hear him asking me questions but how could I answer. Suddenly, I felt cold.

'That didn't last long', I heard him say. I must have been leaning against him as I was aware that he was trying to move me. 'Let me put some money in the meter. Is there a phone in the building? I need to call a taxi you can't stay here the place is running with water.'

'Don't leave me,' I whispered, 'I'm frightened.' Panic hit me as I heard him close the door. I wish he hadn't stopped me I would have been with my mum and dad now if only I had jumped.

I felt him shaking me gently; 'Natasha, Natasha can you hear me? Talk to me please. Where are your clothes? I am taking you away from here. Come on Natasha answer me.'

Did he say he was taking me away? 'All I have is in the large case under the bed. I can't leave I owe the landlord money. Where are you taking me? I don't want to go to the work-house. The landlord said I would end up in gaol. You won't put me in gaol I want to be with my mum and dad; let me die.'

'It's the landlord that needs to be put in gaol no wonder you feel ill the place isn't fit for habitation. Everything is damp even your bedding.' He kept talking to me as he got me to my feet. I felt the room going round and round and then I remember no more.

Through the half closed lids of my eyes I could see the sunbeams dancing; the rays of sun felt warm on my face but I didn't wish to open my eyes as I was so comfortable; where was I? This place was heaven compared to my hovel I didn't want to wake up unless it might all disappear, surely, it was but a dream. Feeling someone holding my hand it was a natural instinct to open my eyes.

'Hello dear; just checking your pulse.'

I closed my eyes whoever it was had spoilt my dream; who was this woman in a royal blue uniform? Then I remembered my last words; perhaps I was in gaol but surely the bed there wouldn't be so comfortable.

'Come, come don't go back to sleep; the doctor said you could sit up today as your temperature is back to normal.'

'Where am I?'

'You have been very ill; been touch and go. I am one of your nurses; Sister Roderick.'

'Am I in hospital?' As soon as I said the words I realized how stupid I must have sounded as on looking around the room I could see nothing but Edwardian splendour. Beautiful chintz drapes hung on the windows and two bedroom chairs were upholstered in the same material; my eyes focussed on the pictures that hung on the opposite wall; I could just envisage walking down the country lane and running through the cornfields.

'No. Come, come; no going back to sleep; come now, time for your medicine.'

I began to recall other moments when I had been given medicine; of seeing two men standing by my bed one holding me in his arms whilst the other appeared to be listening to my chest. Who was the man who held me in his arms? The more I thought about him his image came clearer it was the man with the scar; then it all came flashing back; he was the one who had taken me from that dreadful place; but I still didn't know where I was. Surely this wasn't his home.

'Good afternoon Sir as you can see the patient is so much better today. Doctor Giles said she could sit up for a short while as long as she is kept warm.'

'Hello Natasha'. I hadn't heard him come into the room and when I turned my head I looked straight into his eyes. I saw no scar; all I could see was the handsome man whom I now recalled saved me from that terrible place.

'We have been so worried about you.'

'How long have I been ill and where am I?'

'You are in my London home and you have been here for quite some time. Would you like to sit by the window?' Without waiting for a reply he lifted me from the bed as if I was a small child; he gently put me to sit on one of the armchairs and wrapped a rug around me.

I hadn't done anything but I felt exhausted. I wanted to go back to the comfortable bed and go back to sleep. Memories were continually coming back to me; I recalled being fed broth by a short, grey haired elderly woman and being lifted from the bed by a large, whiskery man who looked like Father Christmas; closing my eyes more visions came fleeting back. Whenever I had opened my eyes he had been by my bed; sitting holding my hand or smoothing my fevered brow. I remember feeling so hot as if my whole body was on fire and then so cold as if I was in the frozen lands of the Artic and when I had tried to move every bone in my body ached.

'Why is it everything about the last weeks so vague?'

'You have been very ill; I don't know what would have happened to you if I hadn't chanced upon meeting you on New Year's Eve. Because you were so weak you were in a comatose state and the medication you have been given has also sedated you to prevent the severe bouts of coughing.'

'Can I go back to bed?'

'A little longer every day until you get your strength back.' As he spoke he picked me up in his arms; how lovely it felt I would love to have been cuddled longer. The nurse put an extra pillow under my head and the rug he had put around me still covered my legs. 'I'll see you later.'

As if someone had just turned on a tap tears flooded from my eyes; I didn't want him to go but deep down there was another reason for my anguish.

'Why the tears little one? Shall we have afternoon tea together; would you like that?'

I nodded my head but there was no comforting me. He sat down on the side of the bed; 'Have you got a headache? It has all been a bit too much for you today but you will soon feel so much better.'

'I don't want to feel better; I don't want to go back to that place.' My sobs were uncontrollable and the more I thought about going back to that dingy flat the more I cried.

'Oh! my sweet; you silly Billy no-one is sending you back there; Ma and Pa Taylor would have something to say about that. Between us I think they have adopted you. Did I see just a glimmer of a smile?'

'Are they your mum and dad?'

His laughter echoed around the room; 'they might as well be but I just refer to them as Ma and Pa as they look after me and my home and I don't know what I would do without them. Now go to sleep and dream about when you are better I might even have need for a secretary'.

Comforted by his words I settled down to sleep; the bed had been freshly made but still wrapped around my legs was the soft fluffy rug; as I turned over onto my side I gently pulled the rug and like a child with its comforter I held it in my arms; it was like holding part of him close to me.

Once I began to feel strong enough everything seemed to happen so quickly. He kept his promise and soon I was sitting in his study typing up the manuscript of a novel he had been writing about the war that had just ended. The more I typed the more I began to wonder was it about the part he had taken; as to me it didn't appear to be fiction.

I was breakfasting alone one morning, as William was on one of his business trips, when Ma Taylor came into the room wearing her hat and coat.

'Go and get your coat we're having a shopping trip to town. His Lordship suggested that you need a new wardrobe of clothes.'

I will mention here that I ignored her reference to 'His Lordship' as mother often had referred to father in the same fashion.

'I can't afford new clothes.'

'You are not paying'; was her comment as she bustled me into a waiting taxi.

Was it my imagination but as we entered the ladies department of the store where a few months previously I had been sacked from I felt as though everyone's eyes were upon me. Then when the floor manager Miss Baxter came to our assistance I really wanted the ground to open up and swallow me. I needn't have worried as it appeared that she hadn't recognized me. Had I really changed that much? I had lost weight and my hair had grown quite long and I now wore it in a neat chignon.

I tried on summer dresses and smart suits and skirts; not all of them bore the utility mark brought in during the early days of the war; shoes, stockings and underclothes the choice was mine; when I hesitated over a summer swagger coat Ma Taylor just ignored me and told Miss Baxter to deliver to our address. I thought we had finished but I was ushered into another room and was told to choose two evening dresses.

Evening dresses for me; I was stunned where was I going to wear an evening dress? Then I thought perhaps William would need me, as his secretary, to go to some special occasion. I chose a black cocktail dress and a vibrant green crepe de chine dress with a knife pleated skirt. I knew that the colour suited my flaming red hair. When William returned a few days later I was like a child showing him my purchases and I just hoped they would meet with his approval. Obviously, I was too coy to show him my French knickers and other underclothes.

We were sitting together after supper that evening when suddenly he got up from his chair and began to walk back and fro. I felt something was amiss; had I bought something that he didn't like?

Finally he spoke, 'Natasha I have a confession to make. I suppose the best way is to be straight with you.'

This sounded so ominous.

'The store you bought your clothes and where you once worked is owned by my family and I have to admit that it was my policy to replace female staff working in the men's departments with the men returning from the war. Obviously it was up to the head of department to make the final choice but I felt so guilty when I realised that losing your job had caused you such heart-break.'

I was taken aback and for a moment I said nothing but then my thoughts turned to what he had done for me,

'William that is all forgotten without your care I would surely have died.'

'When I heard your story I felt it was I who had caused your suffering. I have another confession to make but I wonder is it the right time.' He sat back down in the chair opposite me and lighting his pipe it was a few minutes before he spoke.

I loved these evenings we spent together; sometimes almost in silence. William reading his paper, smoking his pipe and perhaps pouring himself a glass of brandy. I was content.

'Is this second confession so upsetting that you have had to have a second brandy?'

'No. No, I just don't know how you will react. From the moment I saw you across the room at the New Year's party I felt drawn to you; you looked so sad and lonely just the same as I was feeling at that time. Then you smiled and your smile melted my hurt and when the clock struck twelve I just had to kiss you; all be it on the cheek. You looked into my eyes and to me it was if you did not see the scar on my face. I wanted to get to know you better so when you rushed from the hall I just had to follow you. Obviously, the rest you know but one thing you don't know is that while I sat by your bed when you were so ill I fell a little more in love with you each day and then when you were better and said it was time you left I just had to do something to keep you and that was to make you my secretary. Now I have said it; Natasha I love you.'

It was my turn to be lost for words; so I just said the first thing that came to mind. 'So, you really don't need a secretary?'

'I most certainly do as I am hopeless using the typewriter. Natasha, have I spoke out of turn?'

'No; it is my turn now to confess. I think that I fell in love with you when you put money in the gas meter to keep me warm. When I was ill I remember opening my eyes and you seemed always to be there holding my hand or smoothing my hair.'

He put out his pipe and came and sat on the sofa with me. I don't recall who moved first but I found myself in his arms and his lips were upon mine; it was the first romantic kiss I had ever had. To me it was better than anything I had seen in the movies he was my Rett Butler and I was Scarlet O'Hara. His kisses sent a shiver down my spine and brought to life hidden passion that had never before been brought to life.

Although it was almost the end of July a fire still burned brightly in the hearth. We sat watching the glowing embers; he still had his arm around me and I was content to be nestled close to him with my head on his shoulder.

'Why did you want me to choose two evening dresses?'

'I have tickets for the newly founded Covent Garden Opera Company and I would like to take you. The performance is Purcell's The Fairy Queen.'

If William and my relationship was going to grow I must learn to enjoy his lifestyle and educate myself. I was from humble roots and by the way William lived I knew I had a lot to learn.

On the afternoon of the theatre visit a phone call by Ma brought a hairdresser to the house. I had never been so pampered. My hair was pinned, curled and coiled in the fashion worn my most of society; I felt glamorous but I still preferred my hair loose in uncontrollable curls. My nails were manicured and buffed and then when I finally slipped on my green dress over my flimsy underwear I really did feel like a movie star. I was quite tall so the shoes I wore were higher than I was used to with an ankle strap and decorated with a large bow on the front; with my slim figure I looked even taller; in fact, I felt quite elegant.

William's admiring look and the words he whispered in my ear; 'I love you,' gave me the confidence I needed. I must admit I thoroughly enjoyed the performance but as we were leaving a photographer who had been taking photos of groups of people and some celebrities suddenly turned and snapped a photo of us. Over the chatter in the foyer I didn't quite hear what William said but he appeared quite annoyed as he hustled me to a waiting taxi. He said very little as we driven back home. I thought we would sit together for a while and discuss the evening's performance but William kissed me lightly on the cheek and said 'Goodnight'. It was as if I was a naughty child and to me the evening had been spoilt.

I cried myself to sleep that night. I had no reason to be upset I had done nothing wrong but I was upset by William's attitude. Then I thought perhaps he was upset by the photographer taking a photo of the scarred side of his face.

When William was home we always took breakfast together; as I entered the breakfast room William was already seated by the table. 'Good morning sweetheart,' I said placing a kiss on top of his head. 'Did you sleep well?'

Before he had time to reply Pa brought the morning paper. Everything seemed to happen so suddenly. William took one look at the front page threw the paper across the room and stormed from the room.

I never bothered to read the paper but on this occasion as I bent to pick it up the headlines hit me. There was the picture of William and myself but it was the headlines that hit me. *'Who is the mysterious redhead seen with Lord William at the performance of the Fairy Queen? Some starlet after his money he has very little else to offer. She is the talk of the society pages today.'* I didn't bother to read further; I threw the paper on the chair and left the room. I guessed he would have gone to his study; I usually tapped on the door before entering but I just turned the knob and went in. William was sitting with his head in his hands; why was he so upset about the picture and the article? I just went and put my arms around him; 'Why are you so upset? The article doesn't bother me.'

'I haven't been truthful to you from the very beginning; I didn't tell you about the store and there are other things I neglected to mention. I kept them from you because I wanted you to love me for myself not for my family name. I've had many parents trying to marry me off to their daughters who in turn would kiss me and say that my scars and my lame leg didn't bother them but I knew they were lying. I shouldn't have 'tested' you I should have trusted you as I knew from the beginning you were different. I love you Natasha and I must admit I've been beastly.'

'When I look at you all I see in your eyes is kindness and love. I would love you if you were the store-man in the depot. You should have trusted me but I know you have been hurt; not just being let down by the women who chased you but more so by the time you served in the war. The words I am typing for you they are not fiction it is just as it happened to you. Cast it away William; I love you.' Just to make light of the situation I added; 'should I refer to you as Lord or Sir?'

'It is my father who is the Lord and hopefully he will remain so for many years. I think I may insist that you refer to me as Major William.'

The seriousness of the moment had passed.

'You have never mentioned your parents.'

'Sorry, my love I kept it from you because I knew by mentioning them I would have to divulge more facts. I'll take you to meet them I know they will love you. When I am not here I am with them on the family estate in Sussex.'

'The Soviet Union isn't a favourite topic in Britain at the moment; perhaps your parents will be wary of me because I am partly Russian.'

'Don't be silly you were born in this country you are as British as I am.'

The morning that started badly ended with kisses and cuddles that might have gone further if the telephone hadn't rung. Saved by the bell but I was beginning to feel I didn't want to be saved I wanted to be his; completely.

With every passing hour the week-end was getting closer; I was so nervous at the thought that I was completely off my food which in turn worried Ma Taylor.

'I'll cook you a lovely scrambled egg on hot buttered toast.' Ma always kept the 'best butter' as she referred to it, for me.

I couldn't confide my worries to William as he had been with his parents for the last fortnight. I kept remembering the last time we had been together and how both our emotions had almost reached the point of no return; if only the phone hadn't rung. What would it be like? I really was ready to give myself completely to him; I loved him so much but still couldn't quite acknowledge how someone like William could love me; 'a nobody'.

William had kept in touch with a daily phone call; usually ringing just as I was getting ready for bed. His words were loving but he seemed to refrain from saying too much.

'Should be with you early afternoon on Friday; be ready as I'll just grab a quick snack. Get a taxi and go to the store and ask for Miss Baxter; I have spoken to her as I want you to choose a few evening dresses.'

'But William I already have two; surely they will suffice?'

'Special occasion; keep in mind that I love you in the green. Love you.' The phone clicked I had had so much to say and still it lay bottled up. Why was he doing this? I felt like a 'kept woman' but in my case gave nothing in return just those few hours when I acted as his secretary. I trusted him, but I kept having horrible feelings that I would have to 'pay for it' one day.

Miss Baxter welcomed me to the store and soon we were looking through the racks of beautiful evening dresses; all seemed too sophisticated for me. I was tall but couldn't envisage myself in the straight tight fitting sheath like dresses. Then my eyes caught sight of a beautiful black dress on a mannequin.

'I like that dress Miss Baxter but feel I am too young to wear black.'

'I haven't put it on display but I do have it in a lovely shade of green it has exactly the same bronze starburst trim.'

It was divine; I felt like a Greek Goddess. An 'A' line dress with a flattering overskirt; a fitted waist and the draping coming from pleated darts each side creating fabulous shaping at the hips; a concealed side sip and a keyhole opening with a button at the back of the dress. I would describe it as moss green and the fabric a beautiful crepe de chine. What added to its elegance was a front slit from knee to ankle; perhaps a little daring for me but I kept in mind that William said it was going to be a special occasion and he wanted me to look divine. What added to the design was the bronze bugle beads around the neckline and the starburst design of sparkling bronze beads and clear bugle beads that caught the lamp-light. I felt like a million dollars.

Miss Baxter kept repeating herself not just with her 'ohs and ahs' but by saying that it was made for me and I must have it.

After the elegance of my first purchase my second was what one might refer to as a 'pretty' dress. It had a shawl collar, just off the shoulder and not to daring to show too much cleavage. A gathered waist and full skirt of tulle over satin finished with a large tulle bow and a flimsy tulle stole. I loved it in pink but Miss Baxter said it wouldn't suit my colouring so I ended up purchasing in it in a sea blue. She also persuade me to add two pairs of linen slacks; 'Ideal for the country' she had said and two twin sets of fine cashmere.

Going back in the taxi the butterflies in my tummy were increasing by every second. Ma had packed my suitcase and had laid out one of my pretty summer dresses. A pale lemon dress with blue forget-me-nots. I heard William arrive and was a little disappointed that he hadn't come to see me but then I recalled that he said he would have a quick snack.

'Ready my love,' he shouted up the stairs. I took one final look in the mirror and was satisfied at my reflection; picked up my handbag and lace gloves and went to join him. I nearly stumbled down the stairs as he stood at the bottom watching every step I took.

'You look beautiful,' he whispered as he kissed me on the cheek. I wanted to put my arms around him; I wanted him to hug me I felt so insecure and dreaded meeting his family.

We hadn't driven far when he pulled into the side of the road on a busy street; 'Will you be okay? Won't be ten minutes just have to pick up something for mother.'

I counted the minutes he was gone my stress getting worse by every second. 'That didn't take long.' I hadn't seen him coming I must have closed my eyes.

Void of any package; I questioned, 'Didn't they have what your mother wanted?'

'All done.' He smiled at me; his smile turned my emotions upside-down. 'Once out of the city you will enjoy the journey.'

The fields were like a patchwork quilt some were golden ready for harvesting and other green with long lush grass; I was taken back to my childhood and Rupert Bear as it gave me the vision of how Nutwood might have really looked; how I would have loved to have run through the grass in the meadows with William and then lay beneath the shade of the old oak tree and made love. The thought of William making love to me was uttermost in my thoughts.

The first glimpse of the sea made me recall childhood days spent with my parents; building sand castles and paddling in the rock pools. They were happy days; I was content now but I wanted to be really, really happy and fulfilled. We drove along the coast at Hasting still showing signs of war defences and on to Brighton.

He stopped the car in a country lane; putting his arm around me he pulled me close; 'Don't be afraid Natasha the family will love you as much as I do.' He kissed me quite passionately. I clung to him; I wanted his kisses to continue.

'As much as I want you Natasha this isn't the time or the place; I want it all to be perfect.'

'I love you,' I whispered.

'I love you too my darling.' He pulled me close. 'See that lovely old house on top of the hill that is my home. We'll soon be there and mother will be waiting with high tea.'

'High tea?' I questioned.

'Yes; as we missed afternoon tea she will have laid on a late tea. Dinner will be at eight.'

Lunch, tea, high tea, dinner all meaning different to me and would take a lot of getting used to.

'Hope you bought some glamorous evening dresses.'

'Do I need to wear evening dress tonight?'

'Yes my dear but keep the best one for tomorrow it is going to be a special evening.'

Oh my! It was a family evening. His parents were delightful; then I was introduced to an elderly aunt who lived in the Manor. His two sisters and their husbands I found lived in cottages on the estate. They were both eager to tell me about their children and I noticed that they both appeared to be pregnant.

'Making up for lost time,' said the one named Penny; 'a lot of catching up to do after hubby being away in the war.'

'Don't mention the war to William,' said his sister Diane.

'I think he is coping well with it now.' I said.

'Well, if you've done that for him no wonder he loves you.'

They both went off giggling like two school girls; what did they know that I didn't.

It was a beautiful August evening and the moonlight made it appear as if it was daytime. We strolled out into the garden.

'You look so beautiful; love the dress the colour brings out the blue in your eyes.'

'I've been told that they are green you had better look more closely.'

The closer look was to kiss me passionately. His hand moved from my waist and caressed my breast. Nothing had ever happened to me like this before; I could not understand the tingling in my body and the urges in my secret places.

'William mother wants a word with you.'

Woops that was another stop signal.

With his arm still around me we went back in doors.

'Brown has just told me that you have put Natasha in the east wing I thought…'

Before she had chance to finish what she was saying William interrupted her; 'That's right mother I will explain at breakfast; think it is time we called it a night as I can see Aunt Lucy has already nodded off. Have a few things to check in my office so will see you all at breakfast. He kissed me lightly on the cheek but I did notice the loving look he had in his eyes. Kissed his mother 'Goodnight' and crossed the hall to his office.

'Our room is next to yours, so come along dear we may as well call it a night Henry has already gone up. I just don't understand that son of ours fancy putting you in that old room.'

'Old room', it might well be but to me it was the height of luxury. I soon made myself ready for bed and exhausted curled up in the soft feather mattress my last thoughts were of lying naked in the long grass with William.

The sunbeams woke me with their kisses; it was going to be another glorious day. Just as I was about to get up there was a tap on the bedroom door and a maid entered carrying my breakfast tray. What luxury; on it was a bud vase with a beautiful red rose and propped against it a note from William.

'Enjoy your breakfast my sweet; sorry I couldn't bring it personally but have things to do. Meet me by the game-keeper's hut at noon; just follow the path from the orchard up the hill towards the wood you can't miss it. I'll be waiting. Love you always W'

I was intrigued; what was he up to? What had he planned?

I bathed and dressed making sure that I looked just perfect. I put on my cream slacks and the pale lemon twin set I had purchased the previous day; I brushed my hair until it was shining and tied it back with a velvet bow; no, that wasn't the look I wanted so I just tied a deep yellow ribbon around my hair and let it hang loose; I donned a pair of flat pumps and by half eleven I was ready; one more look in the mirror just to make sure I would meet William's approval.

I would have loved to have stopped in the orchard and tasted the fruit that hung in abundance on the trees but today I had other things on my mind. I opened a rickety gate and leaving behind the orchard made my way up the hillside. Glancing back I thought I saw Ma and Pa but cast it from my mind as the sun was dazzling my eyes. The closer I came to the woodland the faster my heart was beating; was it because of the climb up the hillside? I doubt it as I knew my excitement was bubbling over. We would be alone; what would happen? We had reached the 'river of no return' on a few occasions but had never taken the final dive into the deep waters of oblivion; now there would be nothing to stop us. For a fleeting moment I closed my eyes and I could see a couple making love in the long grass.

I opened my eyes when I felt his kiss upon my lips; 'what were you dreaming of my love? You were miles away.'

'You;' was all I said. How handsome he looked; he too was wearing light coloured slacks and an open necked shirt with a yellow spotted cravat at his throat. That was such a co-incidence.

With his arm around me we took the final few steps towards the game-keeper's hut but he didn't stop there a few yards further on and underneath the spreading bows of a horse chestnut tree I noticed a picnic was spread out on a huge rug.

'Lunch is served madam;' he jested as he pulled me down beside him. 'Shall we start with the champers?' Champagne; smoked salmon; meat loaf; small, thinly cut cucumber sandwiches everything looked delicious.

'I've left the dessert in the shepherd's hut to keep it chilled as the sun is rather hot today. I thought about bringing the gramophone but I wanted to get away from the family so that I could talk to you.'

'Why is the party tonight special? Is it your parent's anniversary or something?'

The food was delicious; I had enjoyed my breakfast and surely I shouldn't feel so hungry; perhaps it was the country air; the food consumed I lay back on the rug.

'More champagne?' He filled my glass; the bubbles tickled my nose and made me laugh.

'Are you trying to get me drunk?' I picked a blade of grass and began tickling his face as he lay beside me pretending to sleep.

'I think it is time for dessert.' Was all he said and pulling me to my feet led me to the game-keeper's hut. There was another wicker basket on an old wooden table but he didn't head for that instead he pulled back a curtain to reveal a wooden settle bed covered in cushions and a soft fur rug. I had been waiting for him to hold me but when he did it came as a surprise. His hungry lips were upon mine and his hand began to caress my body. He pulled me down on the settle and his kisses became more passionate; my emotions were reaching boiling point what would it be like? Then as quickly as my emotions had risen they fell flat. He pushed me away from him and I could see a look of anguish in his face.

'What is it William? What is wrong don't you want me?'

'I want you more than anything but I am afraid I won't please you. As you know I've been to hell and back; I have been on so much medication that the medics have said it would affect my libido. I saw my doctor a month ago and except for pain killers all medication has been stopped he checked me over and said that everything should now be okay so why my darling am I putting off making love to you?'

'I kissed him and putting my head on his shoulder I said; 'William how would I know what a good lover is? I am a virgin and you are the first man I have ever kissed with any passion. Your kisses excite me; the way you touch me thrills me but now I want to be completely yours. Just relax put everything from your mind except us and if it is to happen it will; no holding back.'

I took his cravat off his neck and undoing the buttons on his shirt slipped it off his shoulders. Then I slipped off my jumper and undoing my bra threw it on the floor. The sight of my young rounded breasts was enough to get him aroused. He pulled me down beside him and his kisses left my lips; his hungry lips upon the back of my neck set my pulse beating rapidly and when he started kissing my breasts I was like a wild animal I wanted more. I fumbled for the buttons on his trousers; then standing up I unzipped my slacks and stepping out of them and my French knickers also discarded he pulled me down on the bed. Naked as the day we were born there was no more fumbling and no more holding back He was the stallion and I was the young filly ready to be broken in; I didn't want his love making to stop I was ecstatic but finally we lay back in each other's arms.

You are mine,' he said 'all mine forever.'

'I feel like *Lady Chatterley* and you are the gamekeeper'.

He laughed; 'What does a young innocent girl know about *Lady Chatterley*?'

'I read about the *Lawrence's* book in the paper; can't be any more exciting than our love making.'

'Let's see what's for dessert.'

'I thought you had just had your dessert surely you don't want more?' I began kissing him.

'Come you little minx let's dine on strawberries and cream and some more champagne.'

Dessert finished and still unclothed I could but not help noticing that my closeness to William had made him ready for me. This time it was even more pleasurable and my moans of rapture echoed through the woodland. We dressed, still with our emotions boiling over and eager to touch each other.

'No; no not again,' he laughed 'it is getting late and we have to get ready for tonight; can't wait to see your dress.'

'You are a big boy,' I teased as I kissed him.

'I aim to please.'

The blankets folded; the baskets filled and stored in the hut we left hand in hand and together we made our way down the hill. William's limp was hardly noticeable. One finally kiss and a cuddle in the orchard.

'Love you so much,' he said.

'William don't think me silly but I feel so different will people be able to tell?'

'You silly Billy. I will come for you about seven in time for pre-dinner drinks.'

In my room I kept looking at myself in the mirror, surely I looked different; my cheeks were flushed and every time I thought of William I experienced a feeling I never had before.

My beautiful dress was hanging up and my undies lay on the bed; I was beginning to learn that one could hide very little from one's maid. Me with a maid was a big joke what would mama have said?

I was ready and waiting for William; I felt like a Princess. The young maid had dressed my hair in coils and had placed a glittering slide on one side. She had told me William's mother had suggested it would match my dress. How I hoped she had approved of my dress; I hadn't wanted anyone to see it but it didn't really bother me as she hadn't seen it on me. The clock chimed seven when William made his entrance and what an entrance; he wore a kilt and all the finery of his family clan. I was awe struck I just wanted to take him in my arms but knew it wasn't the time or the place. All I could do to hide my emotion was to jest as to what he wore underneath.

'Perhaps you will find out later. You look so beautiful my darling,' Taking my arm he led across the landing and down the ornate staircase.

There were people everywhere in the great hall; William introduced me to so many that their names didn't register. I was in Fairyland and soon my Prince would kiss me and I would wake up; then I saw them across the room Ma and Pa Taylor it really must be a special occasion for servants to be invited but hadn't William said he would never think of them as servants. They both kissed me and Ma said I looked a million dollars and Pa winked at me; this embarrassed me as I felt he knew what had happened.

William's father escorted me into dinner and William his mother; I longed to sit next to William but he was sitting opposite me with his eyes constantly fixated upon me and a smile on his lips.

The meal was never ending; I ate very little my mind still upon the lunch we had shared under the branches of the chestnut tree. I smiled sweetly and endeavoured to chat to his sister's husband but to be honest I was in a world of my own; the buzz of chatter was to me like a beehive and for one day only I was the Queen Bee.

The Master of Ceremonies tapped a glass and silence fell upon the dining hall but I wasn't prepared for what followed.

William got up and came around to where I was sitting and kneeling by my chair he took my hand and said; 'Natasha, will you do the honour of being my wife?'

The hush lingered in the hall as everyone waited for my reply; so this is what the special occasion was.

I felt my cheeks flush and my heart was racing and to give me time to regain my composure I bent my head and kissed him. Then I said, 'I will be delighted to marry you.'

'She said 'Yes'' his father said and everyone began to applaud us as William placed a diamond band on my finger in the design of a Russian wedding ring. 'I stopped to get it yesterday on the way here,' he whispered.

'I love it and I love it even more because you chose it.' It was as if we were in the room alone as he kissed me quite passionately.

'Everyone knew except me,' I whispered.

'Come,' he said and taking my arm he led me into the ballroom. The first dance started with us but soon everyone was dancing.

After I had danced with his father and an ancient uncle William took my arm; 'I have a surprise for you.'

'Won't we be missed?'

'They are all too busy enjoying themselves.' He led me back up the stairs; surely he wasn't planning to have his wicked way with me with all those people in the ballroom; not that I would have minded.

'While I have been away from you I have been busy working down here and I just hope it will meet with your approval.'

Instead of going towards the east wing he opened two locked doors that led to the west wing. Switching on lights I was amazed at the splendour that awaited me.

'I have refurbished the wing just for us; a sitting room, dining room and even a small kitchen. There are three en suite bedrooms and one that I hope will be the baby's room.' He smiled the smile I loved to see; 'it will be a pleasure making one what say you?'

'You did all this for me?'

'I have left our bedroom for you to furnish and I expect there will be other things you will wish to add.'

'What about your London home and Ma and Pa I so love it there as I have such fond memories.'

'We'll be spending a lot of time in London and the home will always be ready for us as it is Ma and Pa's home also. So don't worry. Now my beloved the question on everyone's lips is when are we getting married?'

'Christmas,' I said without giving the question any thought.

'So be it; Christmas it shall be.'

'I was going to ask you were you going to come to my room tonight but I can see it is already early morning.'

'Back in London I will share your bed every night and you can take me to the moon and back. I love you so much my beautiful Natasha. Come we must say 'Goodnight' to our guests.'

It really was a White Christmas wedding in the small church on the estate. My dress was layers of glistening organza, the waistline showed off my slender waist and the finishing touches to the sweetheart neckline was a white fur stole. A long train with sparkling crystals was fixed to my hair that was piled high on top of my head in ringlets and William's mother had given me a diamond tiara.

The only person I wanted to walk me down the aisle was Pa who was so proud on that wonderful day and Ma fussed over me like a mother hen. My nerves left me as I saw William in his Scottish regalia waiting for me by the altar; the look of admiration in his eyes and the smile upon his lips melted my very being I just wanted to hug him.

That night when we would be aboard a ship sailing for the Mediterrean I would reveal the secret that lay hidden beneath the many layers of my wedding dress; come July his wish would come true it would give him plenty of time to furnish the baby's room.

'Do you take this man…….?'

'I do,' I whispered but I wanted to shout out, 'Yes, yes, yes. I love him so much.' It is true *'love is the sweetest thing.'*

Val Baker Addicott

When You Wish Upon a Star Dreams really do come true

Hadn't I vowed that I would never go on a coach trip again yet here I was setting off on a four day break to the West Country. I recalled my daughter's words when she had suggested that I was joining the anorak brigade. That would never be the case I was me and would remain so; perhaps more than a little eccentric. I should have been happy to be getting away for a few days but to be honest an aura of gloom had already set in. My fellow travellers appeared to be a friendly group of people but what was already bugging me was the fact that everyone had a travelling companion be it partner or friend and here I was all on my lonesome and to be honest I was feeling lonely. All my dreams of meeting a second 'Mister Right' had gone down the drain. Who in their right mind would want me? I looked younger than my years but was beginning to feel ancient. Some of my companions were older than myself but far more sprightly; I had once walked miles and now found it hard to keep up with the over eighties. 'Why', you may ask did I choose to go on a coach trip if I was so against it? Well, to be honest it had many 'pros'; I didn't drive so as far as I was concerned it was far easier than going by train; the hotel and tours all arranged for you and your luggage was looked after and taken to one's room. I suppose, deep down, I was hoping to meet someone special; one is never too old to dream if that time ever came one may as well shut oneself away.

'Do you need any help?' asked an elderly gentleman as we re-boarded the coach after a stop off at a service station.

'Thank you; I'll be okay.' Two old dears sitting in the front seat spoke together,

'One, two, three up you get you can do it.'

I smiled sweetly but deep down I was angry; okay the first step was rather high but if they could sprightly get on board why couldn't I? Damn the arthritis and all my other bone problems caused by flat feet. 'Flat feet, my foot', I almost laughed aloud at my own quip.

The hotel was fantastic and I had paid extra to have a room with a sea view. How glad I was to slip out of my 'comfortable' shoes long gone were the days of high heels and strappy sandals. It annoyed me a little as how could one look really glamorous in flat 'comfortable' shoes?

Dinner was from seven so I had plenty of time for a lie down before taking a shower how I longed to soak in a luxurious bath of scented bath foam but again that was a 'no, no' that too had been added to the list of 'no can do'.

Make-up applied carefully, my hair looked great and the last thing for me to do after spraying my favourite perfume was to slip into a maxi dress; a cover up for all sins; my swollen knees and ankles and my unfashionable cosy shoes. My dress was plain but my evening jacket made up for the plainness of the dress as it was of black velvet and quit elaborately embroidered with beads and sparkles. Quite 'eye catching' if I say it myself. Picking up my walking stick and my evening bag I left the confines of my room.

So many things might have been different if I hadn't been so aloof; well not exactly aloof but I hate to admit rather shy, I wasn't a 'people person'. I so hoped that I would be given a table on my own. I observed people but wasn't good at joining in table conversation. Passing through the foyer I noticed a gentleman standing at reception; one could but not notice him as he was a giant of a man he must have been six foot four if not more; although a big man one wouldn't have said he was over-weight. Why, might you ask did I pay such attention to him? It was his hair and his beard; I simply loved a man with grey hair and whiskers.

'Is that Father Christmas?' asked a young lad.

I just had to laugh as I must admit he did rather resemble Santa. He must have heard my laughter as he turned and smiled; 'Hello, fancy meeting you.'

Had he spoken to the child or to me? There was something about him that hit a memory in the back of my mind but for the life of me could I bring it to the forefront.

My meal was delicious but the stranger kept dancing before my eyes; perhaps if I sat in the lounge after dinner and ordered a drink I might see him again. I didn't have to wait that long as I was just finishing my dessert when he was ushered to a table at the opposite side of the room. My, he did brush up well he looked so handsome.

He looked across the room and smiled at me and was that a wink or a twitch of his eye? Me, a senior citizen having the feelings of a teenager how stupid. 'Perhaps he will come and talk to me.' My hopes fell flat when he was joined by a much younger, very elegant lady.

Damn and blast what an idiot wasn't it obvious that such a handsome man would have a partner. I pushed back my chair, picked up my bag and stick and left the dining room without a backward glance. No drinks in the lounge tonight I headed for the lift and my room and bed. Before retiring I sat in the comfortable chair by the window and gazed out upon the stillness of the night; the sky, the sea all looked so dark but as I gazed I noticed the stars lighting up the sky; one in particular shone more brightly than all the others; *'star light; star bright; the first star I see tonight; I wish I may, I wish I might, Have the wish I wish tonight'*. If only wishes really did come true.

The sun was rising in the eastern sky when I finally fell asleep. Who was the handsome stranger? Still at the back of my mind was the fact that I felt I knew him. Going over and over in my mind I tried to recollect people I had met over the last few years and as I said it took until well past four o'clock to hit the nail on the head. It was a case of doing a Sherlock Holmes; elimination. I crossed out people I had met on other coach trips; people I knew through my family and people I saw regularly in the town where I lived this left me with only one other place the local hospital. I tried to visualize doctors and specialists I had met; then the penny dropped; I had met him when my orthopaedic specialist was on sick leave but that was two years ago surely he wouldn't remember me; one reason being that even on that occasion I was treated by a young doctor. How lax of me not even to remember his name. We only met one further time and that was a few weeks later when I literary bumped into him; I think I might have fallen over if he hadn't put his arms around me; had he held me a moment too long and perhaps too tightly. Now closing my eyes I recollected the look in his eyes and the boyish grin. 'We must stop meeting like this', he jested before letting me go; 'sorry about that I was in a rush have a train to catch.'

'No harm done,' had been my feeble reply. I turned to look at him and at the same time he also turned and I noticed he was still smiling. My heart had missed a few beats at that time so why had I put him from my mind completely? I had asked my consultant who the bearded doctor was but he was very negative with his reply. 'That will be Ross; he came out of retirement to help us out.'

So although I now knew where we had met I still didn't know if 'Ross' was his Christian name or surname but at last my brain let me go to sleep.

The day began with an early breakfast as the coach was leaving for our trip to Land's End and other tourist 'hot-spots' en route. My eyes had scanned the dining room but there was no sign of him; I really must put him out of my mind. I was texting my daughter when I felt a presence looming above me.

'Good Morning where did you disappear to last evening? I was going to ask you to join me in the lounge.'

'Your wife would have had something to say about that.' I didn't expect the response that came from my statement. His laughter echoed around the room causing many to glance our way.

'Wife? I have no wife and before you ask I never have had a wife. If you had waited you would have seen her go and join her husband and family.'

I really felt embarrassed; 'I really must be going the coach leaves in ten minutes.'

'Dine with me tonight; I'll meet you in the lounge at seven.'

Why was he making me feel like a silly school-girl? Nothing I said appeared to make sense. 'I'd love to but my meals are already paid for.'

'We'll get round that; seven in the lounge okay?'

I pushed back my chair; picked up my stick and bag and as I passed him he put his hand on my shoulder; 'If I didn't have an appointment today I would have joined you on your day out.'

'See you tonight at seven,' I said as I hobbled out of the dining room. My foot had pins and needles but what made it worse was that I could feel his eyes watching me; I dare not look back.

I enjoyed my day out; the day was sunny but the wind was quite cold as I stood looking out at the blue, blue sea it was hard to distinguish where the sky met the ocean; Land's End; next stop America. I tried to imagine how the land must have once looked before it was commercialized; rugged and open to the elements.

Cornwall made one think of another era and pirates and smugglers.

Back on the coach my thoughts again turned to Ross why was he interested in me? I text my daughter and mentioned that I was having dinner with a most handsome gentleman.

'In your dreams.' She text back.

Okay, leave it at that whatever I say she wouldn't believe me.

Why was I behaving like a teenager on a first date? I had changed three times and a pile of discarded clothes were thrown on the bed. As I began to re-hang them in the closet I noticed a pretty maxi-dress that as yet I hadn't worn. I slipped it on; touched up my make-up and as I picked up my bag I glanced at myself in the long mirror; I might have been standing too close but whatever the reason I was not content with my appearance as the dress clung to my rear making me look far bigger than I really was. I was beginning to get all hot and bothered and time was ticking by it was almost seven o'clock. I grabbed a pair of black palazzo pants and a brightly coloured Aztec design tunic top. I felt good as it covered a multitude of sins but how I wished I had been able to put on a pair of high heeled shoes but alas those days were long gone. Changed the colour of my lipstick to a flash of ruby red; another spray of my favourite perfume and then I ran my fingers through my hair and I was ready. I kept looking at my watch as I waited for the elevator; I was going to be late.

He was waiting by the bar; my heart missed a few beats and my temperature also rose a few degrees; he looked so handsome. 'Do you fancy a cocktail?'

Don't know if I was trying to be clever as my knowledge of cocktails was limited but I had only that day read an article in a magazine. 'I'll have a strawberry martini,' and as an after-thought I added 'shaken not stirred.' If there had been any tension between us that certainly broke it.

'By the way, I think I had better really introduce myself as I believe you called me 'Ross'. Timothy Ross at your service ma-am. Does the name now 'ring any bells'?'

I felt my colour rising; 'sorry but one of your colleagues referred to you as 'Ross'.'

'Suppose he just omitted the 'doctor'.

'Why should your name 'ring bells'?'

'Let me just say I fell in love with you many, many years ago.'

I was bewildered; I could not recall ever meeting a Tim Ross. 'Sorry, but I really have no idea.'

'If I said 'lanky; lamp-post; bean-stalk or four eyes' would that jog your memory? I kissed you once behind the piano in the class-room.'

I just sat there staring at him; his last statement brought memories flooding back. That kiss; it had been the first kiss I had ever had; in fact, I was quite embarrassed by it the reason being that not only was I very shy but to be kissed by the least favourite boy in the sixth form was not on. 'That couldn't possibly be you; you were….' I was going to say ugly but bit my lip. 'You were so tall and skinny and those glasses you wore and the other girls joked about you. I never knew your real name.'

'We moved away a few months later and I never had the courage to ask you out. I really admired everything about you but at that time I mostly admired how clever you were. After my days at university I met up with a few old school friends and asked about you and when they told me you were married I realised that I had really 'lost you' but how can you lose something you never had?'

'Why have you never married?'

'Heart-broken. Only kidding; just had so much I wanted to do between my career and travelling. I must confess that the first time I saw you my heart missed a few beats.'

'How could you have possibly recognised me that was fifty years ago? Back in those days I too was tall and skinny one cannot say that of me now.'

'Was it really that long ago I feel as if it was only yesterday. Think I had your image engraved on my heart.'

'You are a romantic.'

'Shall we go in for dinner I'm starving?'

Over dinner we chatted as if we had known each other for a life-time. Recollections of our old home town and trying to recall the names of fellow students; some he still knew and I mentioned the few I had kept in touch with. Even in that short time we seemed to learn a lot about each other and appeared to have so much in common.

'Shall we have coffee in the lounge?'

He took my arm and to anyone watching we might appear to be 'an old married couple'.

'The lounge appears to be full I believe there is a convention being held here; I'll just go and ask for coffee to be sent to your room perhaps we can watch a late night movie.'

He had that air about him that gave me the impression he was used to giving orders.

How glad I was that I had stopped to put my discarded clothes away. I went to drawer the curtains but he stopped me; 'It such a beautiful evening just look at the moon's refection on the sea.'

My bright star was still shining for me; I turned away from the window and found myself in his arms; I made no effort to move away but was not prepared for what happened. His kisses were passionate and I could not stop myself from responding. I had been 'starved of love' for many a year and now my body was on fire.

A knock on the door brought us both back to reality; 'Coffee'. I said.

'Champagne', he replied.

The moment of passion had gone but within me was a longing for more but also a fear of how far would it go. My daughter would surely be amused to think that her mother, at her age, was thinking of sex. Surely, it wouldn't go that far?

We sat in two rather uncomfortable easy chairs drinking champagne and watching an old movie. The day had been long and my swollen feet were aching I just wanted to stretch out on the bed but how could I?

'I'm getting a crick in the neck watching the T.V. from here I think I'll go and sit on the bed.'

As soon as I moved he was by my side; 'Let me put these pillows behind your head.'

'You have a great bed-side manner.' I jested.

'Think I'll join you those chairs are not very comfy especially for someone my size.'

I began to panic; 'where was all this leading?'

I could feel the warmth from his body; it was such a comfort just like a lovely big, cuddly teddy bear. As I moved to nestle closer to him he put his arm around me and held me close. 'You know I am in love with you,' he whispered.

I heard his words and kept them close in my heart and fell asleep more content than I had been for a long time.

'Breakfast is served sleepy head', I opened my eyes and almost gasped in amazement; surely it couldn't possibly be morning and he was still in my room; had we really spent the night together? 'As you have a free day I was wondering what you would like to do. That is, if you wish to spend it with me.'

'I would love to spend it with you,' I looked at the breakfast trolley and saw it was laid out for two. Perhaps, it would be best to make a joke of the previous night; 'did you sleep well?'

'The best sleep I have had in years; think I'll make a habit of it.'

I was aware that my pretty top was crumpled and my hair looked more like an 'afro' than the smart hair-cut I had the previous evening. I didn't dare look in the mirror as I was certain I also had 'panda eyes'.

'Must 'pop' to the bathroom.' At least that would give me a chance to wipe the make-up off my eyes and put a comb through my hair.

'Tea or coffee madam?'

'Tea please; if it is Earl Grey just a little milk and no sugar.' I hope he had remembered from dinner my tea preference.

The sun was shining; it was going to be a glorious day; the sky was clear blue except for a few cotton-wool clouds that reflected in the azure blue waters of the bay. There must have been just a light breeze that puffed up the sails of the little boats as they bobbed along the waves; a perfect picture.

'There are a lot of little boats in the bay; I know it is the wrong time of day but it reminds me of that song *'Red Sails in the Sunset'*.

'Would you like to go sailing?' Tim asked.

'No thank you. No way will you get me on the water. Had an awkward experience many years ago and another reason is the fact that I can't swim.'

We sat by the window enjoying our breakfast discussing the day's venue. 'I heard that *Trebah Gardens* is worth a visit.'

'Then we shall do what madam wishes; must go and have a shower and change my shirt as for some reason it has got rather creased; good thing about a beard I don't need to shave. Meet you in the foyer at eleven.' He kissed me on the cheek and as he was about to leave my room he turned and taking me in his arms he kissed me passionately. 'Love you', he said.

His strong arms around me made me feel weak at the knees; his kiss set my emotions aflame; 'Love you too'; I replied. I had said those magic words that I thought I would never say again to any man. It was true; I did love him he was everything I had dreamed of in my ideal man.

I poured myself another cup of tea and sat and watched the boats in the bay and the people already walking along the promenade; some with their dogs;

some taking their morning jog; I smiled to myself when a thought passed through my mind that perhaps I should take up speed walking; it was only a flashing thought as I knew quite well it would take me far too long to get from 'A' to 'B'. I quickly showered; sprayed my body with my favourite cologne; slipped into my new undies; what was I, a senior citizen, hoping for? Put on my slim fit navy trousers and another of my favourite tunic tops a white and navy abstract design. Took my favourite navy 'boyfriend' jacket trimmed with white off the hanger. Transferred my wallet; make-up and bits and bobs into my white '*Kipling*' bag. One last look in the mirror I was satisfied with the image that looked back at me. Picked up my stick and went to meet him.

How easy I found it to make conversation with Tim; the more we talked the more I realised we had so much in common. Sitting by his side as we drove along the country lanes I wanted to reach out and touch him I could feel an aura radiating from him and encompassing me; I felt we were as one.

The panoramic view of the garden; the trees in their summer gowns and the sub-tropical plants was a lot for the eye to take in. We had a lot to thank *Major Tony Hibbert* and his predecessors for. I had read somewhere that one of the oldest trees was a pine planted over 160 years

I didn't want to mention to Tim but by the time we reached the Water Garden my feet and legs were beginning to ache; I knew I couldn't walk any further. 'Shall we sit awhile and take in the view? It must be really magnificent here when the azaleas and rhododendrons in the valley are in full bloom.'

I don't know if the anguish was showing in my face but Tim asked; 'Are you all right?'

I could have cried I had asked to be brought here and now I was going to spoil it for Tim. 'I can't walk any further; it is okay to keep going down but one has to walk back. I don't want to spoil it for you.'

'And I don't want it to be spoilt for you; you sit there and rest I'll go back to the centre as I saw there were wheel-chairs there.'

'But Tim you can't push me in a wheel-chair it will be too much of an effort.'

'Are you saying that I am a feeble old man? Just look at me I am stronger than a lot of youngsters. I'll bring you back a nice cold drink.'

I could feel the warmth of the mid-day sun on my face, it helped me to relax. The water garden was such a beautiful place to sit, it made one feel that one should have brought one's sketch pad. I closed my eyes. I could hear the voices of people passing by but it didn't mar the feeling of tranquility; heaven on earth.

I heard his laugh and then he said; 'Caught you having forty winks. Your snoring has driven away all the birds.'

'I wasn't sleeping I just closed my eyes; the sun is so warm and yet there is a lovely breeze.'

'Jump aboard my lady your chariot awaits.'

'Are you my knight in shining armour?'

'Sir Timothy Ross at your service ma-am; a knight of the realm.'

I felt slightly embarrassed but if we were to enjoy the beauty of the garden together there was no other way. Refreshed with the cold drink and the time resting on the bench I was ready to move on. We passed the Fernery and joined the Beach Path. Taking our time we took in all the magnificence of this beautiful garden, The Gunnera Passage amazed us.

Giant rhubarb' Tim jested. 'One could have a lot of rhubarb pies from that monster 'triffed'.'

'Thinking of your stomach already after the breakfast you ate?'

I loved the hydrangea that grew in my garden but these in the Hydrangea Valley were 'awesome'; such an array of colours mirrored in the waters of Mallard Pond and the bridge that really could have been from Monet's painting that gave such a splendid view.

We were behaving rather immaturely for people our age. On any gradient Tim would suggest that I freewheel to the end. I also reminded him that he would have to push me back and he had joked that he would get a helicopter to air-lift me back. We were having fun and enjoying our special day together; just a little cloud crossed before me it was the thought that tomorrow I was to return home.

We reached the bay; it was hard to believe that during world war two the American's had set up their training base here prior to the D Day landings now aptly named *Yankee Beach.*

We had spent a great deal of the day laughing and enjoying each other's company but Tim's final antic really amused me. To my amazement he sat down took off his shirt and then his shoes and socks and then rolled up his trouser legs. 'What are you doing?' I questioned.

'Going for a paddle to cool my feet down.'

I watched him run down the beach like a youngster seeing the sea for the first time. For a man his age he had a fine physique. Where had my new found emotions come from? Just to see his naked chest sent shivers down my spine. This was an idyllic place to while away an afternoon. I watched his every move I just couldn't take my eyes off him as he walked back up the beach. He began to rub the caked on sand off his feet with his socks and slipped his feet back into his shoes. 'Shall I put your socks in my bag I always carry a carrier bag?'

'Were you a girl guide?' He said shaking his socks before handing them to me.

'Now I am covered in sand.' I rose from the chair and sat down beside him. He pulled me to him and kissed me.

'People are looking.'

'So what;' and he kissed me again more passionately. I could feel the heat of his body penetrating through the flimsy material of my top. Nothing made sense any longer what I thought usually happened to the young was happening to me I could feel my nipples harden; how I wanted this man to make love to me.

Time and tide wait for no man; it was time for us to leave as it would take a while to return to the hotel.

We stopped in the centre for a pot of tea and a piece of cake and then we made our way back to the hotel. On our journey back we both appeared to be in a more pensive mood.

'Sorry Tim that you had to get a wheel-chair I really didn't think that I wouldn't be able to do the walk. We will have to find something more relaxing to do……..'. I was going to say 'tomorrow' but there was to be no tomorrow as I was to return home. I felt very near to tears; 'Tim?'

'What is the matter? You sound upset.'

'I don't want to go home tomorrow.'

'Well, don't then come and stay with me until we can make plans. We'll talk about it at dinner this evening meet you in the lounge at seven. I had better not come to your room or I will never leave.' He opened my room door and gave me a hug. I wanted to rub my fingers through his thick wavy locks; I loved to feel his beard tickle me when he kissed me. I clung to him.

'Away with you; or I will succumb to your magic. I believe you have already put a spell on me. Strawberry martini tonight or do you want to try something different.'

'You choose a cocktail for me.'

I was alone in my room but didn't feel alone as Tim's body odour lingered on my clothes. After asking for a call in time to beautify myself for Tim I lay on the bed and soon fell into a relaxing sleep.

I arrived in the lounge just a few minutes before seven and was disappointed that Tim wasn't waiting for me. I sat in a comfy chair and gazed out at the setting sun that left a red glow upon the sea. The time ticked by so slowly; in my present mood every minute appeared to be fifteen. I was really getting wound up; should I ask them to ring his room? What if he had already booked out? Going through my mind was the old saying about 'holiday romances'. I was very near to tears when I heard his cheery voice.

'Hello, darling sorry I am late. Did try to text you.' He greeted me with a kiss. 'Had important things to do.'

Silly me I had forgotten to check my mobile. Most likely my daughter had also been checking up on me.

'Have told your tour guide you won't be returning with them and have made the necessary arrangement for you to stay with me.'

'Where is your home?'

'You'll see tomorrow. Shall we take a walk in the garden?'

'Our table was booked for seven.'

'All sorted.' He put his arm around me and together we made our way into the garden. It was as if we were in a tropical paradise. The evening was warm but the closeness of Tim beside me made me shiver.

'Surely, you are not cold?' He pulled me closer to him and kissed me passionately. My whole being turned to jelly.

'Shall we sit here and watch the sunset?'

'That sailing boat appears to have red sails as it drifts into the sun's reflection'.

We sat closely together on the garden bench as we watched the sailing boat.

He whispered in my ear: *'Swift wings you must borrow; Make straight for the shore; We marry tomorrow and she goes sailing no more. Red sails in the sunset.* He took his arm from around my shoulders and to my surprise knelt down on the grassy verge. 'My darling Faye, will you do me the honour of marrying me?' He held in his hand a small box and when he opened it my eyes focussed on the most beautiful engagement ring with rubies and diamonds.

I didn't know whether to laugh or cry; laugh at him kneeling before me oblivious of any passers-by or cry with joy that he really did love me.

Why did I hesitate to reply? My imagination was running wild; no longer could I be said to be 'an oil-painting'; far from it as on times I felt more like a relic. If I married him how would I be able to hide my body from him and then the thought of taking our love making to the ultimate conclusion alarmed me as it had been many a year since that had happened.

Tim got up and sat beside me and taking my hand he said; 'Why do you hesitate? At our age time is short we need to make the most of it; we are made for each other. I love you Faye and I want you to be my wife.'

'But....' I hesitated. 'You might not find me attractive.'

He must have guessed my inhibitions as he roared with laughter; 'Just wait until you see me with no clothes on. I am no oil-painting.'

In my eyes he was as I could still picture him on the beach without his shirt. To quote; 'love is blind' perhaps in his eyes I too was beautiful.

'Well, am I to take this ring back to the shop? Took me ages to choose it that is why I was late or do you want me to go down on my knees again?'

I just put my arms around him and hugged him; 'I will be delighted to be your wife.'

He placed the ring on my finger; 'It is beautiful Tim and a perfect fit. How did you know especially with my arthritic fingers?'

'Took this one off your table last evening to make sure.' He handed me back a silver ring that I hadn't even missed. 'Come on 'old girl' let's go and dine.'

As we walked by the pianist Tim stopped and whispered something to him. Half way through our meal the pianist said; 'I will now play *'Love is a Many Splendid Thing'* for a recently engaged couple and we wish them every happiness. How grateful I was that no-one looked at us although we were both brimming over with happiness.

Later that evening I text my daughter to say I was getting married and her reply was; 'Nutter'. Did she really think I was making it all up?

After dinner we walked hand-in-hand across the beach and finding a secluded cove we sat and watched the sun setting. Had we had too much champagne? I felt my youth had returned; my old bones no longer ached as we kissed and cuddled. My breasts no longer felt like those of a mature woman as he caressed my body I felt young and beautiful. The saying 'saved by the bell' wasn't appropriate this time as it was the tide creeping slowly towards us that stopped the inevitable.

'We had better move Tim or we shall be cut off.'

'Plenty of time,' was his reply as his hands and his lips caressed my body.

'I love you Tim but we must move; I want you as much as you want me but I don't want to be drowned.'

'Are you that afraid of the water?'

'I nearly drowned in a park paddling pool when I was a child and I can't swim.'

'I will have to teach you to swim in the sea.' He jested.

'No way, you'll not get me in the sea.'

It was really late; way gone mid-night when we returned to the hotel. Perhaps age had caught up on us as he kissed me 'Goodnight' and returned to his room.

I text my daughter to tell her I wouldn't be returning home for a few days and that I was no 'nutter' as I really was engaged and sent her a picture of my ring. I didn't expect an immediate reply as it was really late.

I slept the sleep of a contented baby knowing that we were to meet at breakfast before he took me to his home for an extended holiday. I had drifted to sleep trying to envisage what his home would be like.

As we walked into the dining room together I noticed that guests were smiling at us; had word already got out that we were engaged. A couple from my coach party stopped me and congratulated us. Were they smiling because they were happy for us or because they thought that we were too old for romance? Little did they know.

I was too excited to dine on 'the full English' and just had cereal and fruit. I returned to my room for a last check that I hadn't left anything behind; it was just by chance that I found my mobile phone plugged in to charge but had forgotten to switch it on. So even if my daughter had tried to contact me it would have been to no avail. The porter came and picked up my suitcase and told me that Mr. Ross was waiting in the foyer. One last look in the mirror and I was satisfied with what I saw. Had love brought out something in me? A new lease of life.

As I stepped from the elevator I saw Tim; my heart missed a beat he was so handsome; a handsome giant and he was mine.

'Your limousine awaits ma-am.'

'How far are we going?'

'A couple of miles.' Tim didn't appear to want to give anything away.

'Do you live in a delightful village with a village green and a duck pond and ye olde world country inn?'

He just laughed and asked how many more questions I was going to ask.

'Think we'll stop for lunch I know a lovely 'ye olde world' country inn.' He jested.

I had been taking note of the road signs but was still surprised when I realised the inn that Tim was planning for us to have lunch was really an old inn as it was *The Jamaica Inn of Daphne du Maurier acclaim.*

Lunch was a lovely relaxed meal; we joked and teased each other and Tim told me tales about smugglers; 'Will you bring me back soon there is so many places I would like to visit.'

'We could spend our honeymoon in *Wookey Hole* with the witches.' On that note we left the Inn and journeyed on; when I saw the signpost for Bude I realised we had travelled north from the south coast of Cornwall. Why was he determined to keep our destination a secret? I began to visualize his home as a villa on the sea front over-looking the channel. How wrong I was; he parked the car close to an inn on the banks of a canal; surely he didn't own a pub?

He came around and opened my door; 'Come on my love we have arrived.' The area was a hive of activity with people walking their dogs and jogging along the tow-path; there was an array of small boats and colourful house-boats; how I loved the colourful barge painting on these crafts.

'Why stop here? It is too early to eat again.'

A young man waved to us; 'Haven't visited us for a while Doctor; will you be dining here this evening?'

'Table for two in the snug about seven.'

I was getting more and more anxious. Where was he taking me?

He took my arm; 'I'll pick up your bags later; hope you are ready for this?'

We walked a short distance along the tow-path and then stopped; 'Hope you like your holiday home.'

I just gazed in amazement; his home was one of the colourful house-boats that were moored on the banks of the canal. I was excited but also full of trepidation as my fear of water filled me with awe. I didn't want to show any disappointment thinking that the canal waters were different than the sea. 'It is beautiful Tim.'

It really was splendid; just like a large static caravan. Everything appeared to be in pristine condition. The fitted furniture in the lounge; the galley kitchen appeared to have never been used. When I mentioned this to Tim he said he always ate in way-side inns. The shower room was compact and I noticed a panel of buttons with instructions of how to flush the toilet. There were two bedroom cabins; one luxurious and a smaller anti room with a bunk bed. 'I'll sleep in there;' said Tim and winked at me.

We walked back to *The Brendon Arms* for our evening meal. We were both in a light-hearted mood; a few young joggers sniggered when they saw us kissing did they really think they had the monopoly on romance? Our evening was just perfect the food, the wine and the real ale that Tim drank all helped to dispel my fear of water and I was quite looking forward to returning to the luxurious house-boat and thoughts of being alone with Tim delighted me; that was until the landlord said that we should be thinking of getting back as there was a storm brewing.

'Blowing up the Chanel should hit us before midnight.'

Taking my case from the car we headed back but before we reached a safe haven we were hit by a heavy shower. The rain didn't deter our feelings; in fact, it brought about a fit of laughter; Tim looked like an English Sheepdog that had just had a bath. 'Are you laughing at me? You should see your hair you look like a Poodle.' He said taking me in his arms. The jollity ended when I heard the thunder and felt the rocking of the boat. 'Think we should hit the sack'.

'Tim I can't sleep on my own I hate the thunder and it even worse being on a boat.' A flash of lightening and I was in his arms.

'I'll just go and check everything you go and get ready for bed.'

Was he being diplomatic? I slipped out of my wet clothes and sprayed my favourite cologne, rubbed my hair dry and removed my make-up. All I could think of was what would he think of me without my make-up and 'yes' I did rather look like a Poodle. I put on one of my more sexy nighties and was just getting into bed when I heard him returning. I almost jumped back out when there was another clap of thunder.

'Warm the bed for me won't be two minutes.'

I switched off the bedside lamp and as I did so the lightening lit up the room. 'Tim'. I yelled. I saw him in the half-light all he had on was his boxers. He was in bed beside holding me in his arms; I nestled into his bare chest but his strong arms could not take away the fear not just of the thunder and lightning and the rocking of the boat but what would happen being so much in love and in such close proximity; our age made no difference we both wanted to fulfil our love.

The storm outside raged for over an hour and gradually the last rumble of thunder faded in the distance but then a new storm began; a storm of passion. While the storm outside had raged he had fondled me and kissed me hungrily and I had caressed his body; foreplay had been enjoyable but that was then now it was time to complete the act of love. He moaned with pleasure and I clung to him and begged him not to stop; I felt like a virgin being broken in. The act didn't last long but the pleasure it brought us exceeded all beliefs; we were one. If the storm was to return it would not disturb us as we slept contentedly in each other's arms.

The time went by far too quickly and I knew that I should return home but I didn't wish to leave Tim. Luckily for me the house-boat had remained moored; we rose late in the morning and settled to sleep in the early hours after a day of sight-seeing. The country-side was so beautiful and so was our relationship it was a time of really getting to know each other.

'I don't want to leave you; will you come home with me?'

'I've been doing a lot of thinking my love; how do you feel about selling up and finding somewhere to live that will be out love nest? I'll sell the house-boat.'

'Think we should keep the house-boat Tim it holds such good memories.'

After a night of love and a lazy morning we decided to visit estate agents as our choice for our new home was to be the West Country. The next day we had an appointment to visit a beautiful house on the out-skirts of the ancient town of Camelford; were we so much in love that everything we saw was just perfect. The agent insisted we saw a further two houses but our heart was set on the first property.

I looked at Tim with amazement when he said that it will be a cash sale. 'No rush to sell yours perhaps we could even rent it out. Now my love everything is just going perfectly just one thing more left to do and that is set the date.'

'Two more things my dear we have to tell my daughter perhaps we should visit her on the way.'

I must admit that I had switched off my mobile as I hadn't wanted anything to interfere with our time together. I charged my phone and then glanced at her messages; firstly it was; 'where are you mother?' Finally; 'Get in touch; worried about you.'

I text her back; 'Sorry love, as usual mis-placed my phone; we will stop off at Bristol on way home so will explain all when I see you on Saturday.'

Text message came back; 'Glad you are okay was worried; who is 'WE'?'

'See you Saturday – early afternoon.'

My daughter and her family adored Tim and when a few miles further we finally reached my home there were a few raised eyebrows from the neighbours when they realized that their elderly neighbour had brought a man home with her. We heard the rumours that he was a long lost brother but my close neighbour soon put that right when she saw the ring on my finger and I introduced her to Tim.

'Ten of the Best'

As cash buyers everything moved really quickly and we planned to move by early September; I was already visualizing Christmas with my family in our new home; just one thing was causing Tim strife and that was the fact that I hadn't set a date. I just felt we were happy as we were and couldn't visualize myself as a bride at my age.

Tim had gone to a meeting in Bristol and I was busy packing and feeling my years. We were to move in ten days; I took a break and noticed a message from my daughter; 'Will you and Tim come for the week-end? Buy something new; way-out knowing you, hat as well as we are going to a very posh garden party. Won't take 'no' as an answer.' I thought that Tim would say it would be too close to moving but he appeared to be all for it and was even prepared to go shopping with me the next day.

'Good to have a break; lunch in town we'll make a day of it.'

Things about Tim still amazed me; he insisted on taking me to the most expensive fashion shop and when I started looking at dark floral or abstract designs on maxi dresses he had suggested that it was a summer garden party and I should have something light.

With his persuasion I finally settled on an ivory dress accentuated with a border of blush pink rose buds and trailing foliage; crossed over at the bust that luckily didn't show too much cleavage and short cap sleeves. I noticed Tim chatting amiably to the assistant who then came and asked would I like a lace ivory shawl just in case the day got chilly. Finally the hat and with a great deal of persuasion I succumbed to their suggestions of a blush pink straw with a full blown rose and a few fluffy feathers. I must admit I felt good; just one problem my shoes. Tim put my mind to rest by saying that no-one would see my feet. I was also beginning to wonder how 'posh' a do it was going to be.

There appeared to be great excitement at my daughter's home with regards to the forthcoming garden party but there was a damper put on this when late on Friday evening Tim said he had had a message that the moorings on the house-boat were insecure and would he travel to Bude; 'I may as well stop over as it will be late. Be back in time for the 'do'. He gave me a kiss and a hug and left.

A night on my own; how funny it felt I really missed Tim by my side in bed; how I loved cuddling up to him and the saying of 'absence makes the heart grow fonder', was really true even though it had only been one night it made me realize how much I loved him. Perhaps, I should set the date of our wedding.

I sat in the garden room having a late breakfast. Everyone seemed to be so busy; friends of Rowena's had called; the two teenage grand-children came and gave me a hug and then disappeared with 'see you later'. My very pregnant grand-daughter and her husband arrived. I hadn't seen her since their wedding and was a little disappointed that she didn't stop to chat. 'Things to do for the garden party; we'll catch up later.' Hustle and bustle; comings and goings. Oh! For the quiet idyllic life with Tim. I had a brief text message from him; 'Love you. Will meet you at the garden party.'

I must have dozed off; a bad habit with the elderly!!!

'Come on mum time to get ready.'

'Is it time for lunch?'

'You had a late breakfast thought we would manage today; it is time you put on your 'glad rags' for the garden party.'

I noticed that she was already dressed in a dusky pink and grey maxi skirt and jacket. 'You look lovely,' was my comment.

Fussed over by my daughter my make-up was done and my hair that I usually just put a comb through was back-combed and sprayed with lacquer something I never used. 'All this fuss for a garden party are we going to meet the Bishop and all the 'big wigs'?' Finally I slipped on my dress and a pair of cream 'comfy' shoes. Put on my hat at a jaunty angle and picked up my bag that just contained the necessities.

The sun was high in the sky and as we travelled down a leafy country lane it flickered through the foliage. 'At least the sun is shining for this posh garden party; what it is in aid of?'

'Be there now in five minutes;' was her only reply.

'Thought Bob was driving.'

'He's taken the other car.'

Giggles came from the grand-children.

I noticed a small country church and a marquee in an adjacent field but observed that there were only a few cars parked on a verge. Perhaps we were early.

Rowena parked alongside her husband's car. 'No nonsense from you two; go and find your father.'

'Where's everyone?' I questioned.

'We had better go and check; come along mum take my arm you don't need your stick.'

'A fine mess we'll be in if I fall over and pull you with me.'

'Leave it mum'.

Waiting in the porch was Olivia her pregnancy was bringing out the best in my beautiful grand-daughter. She grabbed my bag and picking up a bunch of pink rosebuds and baby's breath handed the bouquet to me.

'Everyone's waiting granny dear.'

As Rowena took my arm Olivia opened the door and the strains of the organ filled my ears. There appeared to be quite a gathering of people but my eyes only focussed on my beloved Tim; he was wearing a grey suit and in his lapel he wore a rose the same as in my bouquet.

'Who planned this?' I whispered to Rowena.

'Tim and I we were fed up of waiting for you to set a date.'

'Love you,' I whispered to her.

I handed my bouquet to Olivia as I took my place by Tim's side.

'Who givest this woman…..'

Rowena said 'I do'.

Just the touch of Tim's hand sent a tingle down my spine. I could not hear the words but I could read his lips; 'I love you'.

It had been a whirlwind romance but on our wedding day I knew that it would be an everlasting love; the beginning of our life together for as many years as God would give us; two senior citizens happy in each other's love; making each hour a day and each day a week and each week a year; a lifetime of happiness.

That night we lay together in our hotel room the curtains of the window left un-drawn; the moon's light shone upon our honeymoon bed and my lucky star twinkled brightly in the heavens. My wish had really come true.

The End

Val Baker Addicott

Merlin

I closed my eyes and the vision I saw brought to me great happiness; I was sitting at the feet of my beautiful mother, who was nonchantly twisting my ebony ringlets through her fingers; I wore a beautiful blue broiderie anglaise dress and a had a large satin bow of ribbon in my hair It was one of those golden, halcyon days of a summer now long gone but one that would always remain in my memory. Mother was so beautiful; father always referred to her as his Dresden China Doll; her skin was like fine porcelain and to protect herself from the summer sun she sat on the garden bench under a parasol that gave her protection from the sun's strong rays. The view was panoramic; as from our large home and grounds we had a beautiful view of the Cornish coast. Father came striding along the lawn; he appeared, to me as a child, to be so tall and handsome in a rugged kind of way. He bent over and kissed mother and placed in her hand a single red rose; 'shouldn't you be resting, my sweet?' He questioned.

'Do not worry so my darling I will rest later when Vi has her music lesson.'

I guessed that father was concerned about mother as I had been told that I would be having a baby brother or sister when the summer was over and I was to return to school. There were so many things that I didn't understand; I had heard mother and father talking to the doctor and he had been telling mother to 'take things easy' as she had 'lost' two babies; how could one lose a baby?

The scene changed; like a mist on Bodmin Moor, it was a dark, ominous cloud that blotted out the sun. Father had sold our grand home and we now lived in a squalled place near Penzance; I no longer wore pretty dresses and now my beautiful hair was matted and tangled. The change had taken place after mother had died giving birth to my baby brother; they had both been buried in the church-yard near Tintagel. Father was broken hearted and he took to consoling himself in drinking liquor. He got into bad company and began to gamble and within a year we had to sell the house. It had been a long arduous trek to Penzance but father said he knew some-one who would give him work. There was worse to follow; one afternoon, when I was about thirteen, father brought home a gentleman; I assumed he was a gentleman as he was dressed in fine clothes like father once wore.

'Vi always remember that mother and I loved you so much;' his words upset me as he hadn't mentioned mother since the day of her burial and had hardly spoken any kind words to me from that day; he continued, 'you are going to live with Mr. Murphy he has kindly offered to employ you as scullery made.' I could see that father was trying to hold back tears.

'I don't want to go and live with Mr. Murphy I want to stay with you.'

'Get moving child I haven't got all day;' he pushed me towards the door.

'Treat her well Shaun.'

'I paid you well for the brat by cancelling your debts to me; she is mine now and I can treat her as I wish; get out of my way,' again he pushed me; harder this time that I nearly fell. 'Don't get yourself into more trouble;' was his last retort to my father; 'I won't be there to help next time.'

We travelled for what seemed miles in his fine carriage; I had started to cry but refrained from doing so as he had kicked my leg with his riding boots. When we did finally stop it was outside a fine mansion and I heard that we were not far from Truro. From that very moment I was treated badly, how I longed to return to my father. I was more or less dragged into the kitchen by the coachman.

'The Master said to feed the brat and then shove her in the room above the stable until he decides what he is going to do with her.'

That cloud stayed with me and seldom did it allow the sun to shine through. I worked as a scullery maid and did all the dirty jobs that no-one else wanted to do. I had a meagre ration of food and was beaten by the housekeeper if she saw me idling. When I first started my cycle I was frightened that I was dying yet it brought relief to me that it would be the end of my life of terror but a maid told me it was natural and it was a sign that I was becoming a woman and advised me to stay away from dirty old men or I would end up in the work-house. I understood very little of her explanation. At that time each month the house-keeper was even crueler as she would lock me away in my stable room until the period had stopped. All I had was straw on the floor and a few old sacks that gave me very little warmth on cold winter nights and a bowl of icy cold water to wash and a bucket.

Almost three years I suffered this torture; for that is what it was. It was a hot day at the end of summer when I was sitting in the yard cleaning all the dirty boots when I overheard an argument.

'If I want to 'take' you in the afternoon I bloody well will.'

'The baby Shaun you might harm the baby; my time is near.'

I heard my Mistress scream out; I was naïve as the day I was born; no-one had told me what went on between man and woman. What had the master done to make his wife scream so loudly?

'You fat bitch,' he yelled, 'if you can't satisfy me I'll get young Vi in my bed she is ripe for the picking; there will be fun and games then after I have broken her in.'

His words rung in my ears and I recalled what the maid had said about staying away from 'dirty old men.'

I made up my mind there and then that I was going to 'run away'; but where could I go? Then an idea flashed across my mind; I had heard the stable boys talking about a circus that was in town and they were going to go on the final Saturday before it upped-sticks and moved onto the next town. I had remembered going to the circus with mother and father and they had said that the circus people were 'travelling folk' and I remembered father jesting that as a boy he always wanted to 'run away' and join the circus. Today was Sunday and in the distance I could see the trail of caravans moving along the highway. They would surely pass by about a mile from where I was now standing. I ran to the stable rolled up in a sack a piece of stale bread that I saw lying on the stable floor and a handful of oats that was the horses feed and from which I had ate for quite some-time. The only possession I had was a photo in a silver frame of mother, father and myself taken at Christmas-time a year before mother died; this I had kept well hidden. I glanced around and it appeared that everyone was busy; the family visiting friends after Sunday Mass; Sunday Mass that in itself was a joke to me as I wondered what the priest would have said if he knew how they were treating me. I hadn't been inside a Church since mother's funeral; we always went as a family every Sunday and often lunched with the vicar and his wife and family; those were such happy days; would I ever be happy again?

I started off at quite a brisk pace but the further I walked I began to slow down; my feet hurt and I could see that they had begun to bleed as the thin leather on the sole of my shoes had worn away and there was a big hole in the bottom. Obviously, the slower I walked the further into the distance the circus seemed to disappear. It was getting quite late; 'surely', I thought they would stop for the night and then I would be able to catch them up. 'It must be early evening', I thought as the sun was sinking fast in the west. The evening came upon me so quickly as one minute there was a cloudless sky and the next the sky became grey and overcast. I had no idea of where I was and I could no longer see the circus; I had been following what my father would have called a 'sheep track' quite a distance from the road and now I began to wonder had it veered further away; I saw a few sheep grazing and in the distance some ponies how I wished that I could catch one and not have to walk any longer. I was so tired and although I saw sheep I could not see any sign of a farmhouse or shepherd's hut. The terrain that had once been rough beneath my feet now began to feel marshy and along the edges where there had been heather and grass there now grew reeds. If only I could find a place to shelter until morning then a new day would bring better views of how the land lay. I kept stumbling over my own feet but managed to keep going but then I tripped over something on the path and felt myself rolling down a bank; I tried to pull myself back up but each time I appeared to slip further back. I had had enough, if no-one came along the path I would die and be in heaven with my beloved mother; that would most certainly be better than the life I had in servitude. Thinking of my mother made me cry and I recollected her words 'that life was precious'. If I lay still perhaps I could sleep and with a new day find a way to get out of my predicament. A mist had fallen and seemed to shroud me as it swirled about. If there were reeds and such wet earth surely I must be nearing the shore; could the circus have been heading for St. Austell? I tried again to pull myself up from the hollow by crawling forward on my hands and knees I didn't slip back this time but exhausted collapsed.

    I felt myself being lifted up; had the angels ascended and were carrying me to heaven but on opening my eyes I screamed. It was the devil himself who was carrying me off to Hades; had I been that wicked that the angels weren't sent for me. In the glow of a lantern I saw a being in a dark cape and a large black hat; very little of a face was visible as it appeared to be on fire.

'Well, Ned what have we found here?'

My fear calmed a little when I saw the horse and the fire on the man's face; for that is what he was; was just his 'red' beard and whiskers. His voice was also soothing and comforted me as he sounded like father.

'Did you get left behind by the circus lass?'

'No' I whispered; 'I was running away from my master and was trying to catch up with them but I was too slow and lost sight of them.'

'You poor little one; you have wandered miles from the main route to St. Austell where the circus was heading. It was a good thing that you did stumble because the path you were taking would have led you into the marsh and the lake and there are also many treacherous areas that would have sucked you down.' He put me down in the back of the trap and taking off his cape put it over me. 'I'll take you to my humble abode and in the morning we will journey on to my sister who lives in Newquay. What shall I call you little one?'

'My name is Vi; father said that mother was such a romantic that she named me Viviane but I have always been called 'Vi'.

The man roared with laughter; why was my name so funny?

'I am known as 'Merlin' I believe my little Lady of the Lake we were fated to meet.'

I knew well the Arthurian legends as mother had often related them to me; was my rescuer really Merlin the Magician?

'I am known locally as Captain Red Davies as I travel the vast oceans and seldom spend time in my home.

He called to the horse; 'Home boy' and I felt the movement of the trap rock me into a dream like stupor. I pulled his cloak over my shivering shoulders and nestling my face into the course fabric I could smell his masculine odour. It made me feel safe; it seemed to cast a spell over me and gave me the feeling that this man would not harm me. How had he found me? He had appeared, as if by magic, from nowhere. If he had been travelling behind me surely I would have noticed him but there again perhaps not as the mist had come down quickly and visibility had been poor. What if he hadn't found me would I have endeavoured to continue on and be sucked down in a peat bog? I must have fallen asleep as when I opened my eyes I was being lifted from the trap and Merlin was calling out to someone called Zac to take the horse to the stable. The moon was high in the sky so I guessed we must have travelled some distance. As he strode across the yard realization dawned on me that every bone in my body was aching and the worse hurt were my feet.

'Jesse', he called get the kettle on 'I found a wee lass lost on the moor.'

I wondered was Jesse his wife; I didn't want him to have a wife so hoped that Zac was her husband. Merlin was my knight in shining armour and as I nestled close to him my heart began to beat faster.

He put me down on what appeared to be a bed in a cupboard and from there I could see a roaring fire in the hearth and on the table an oil lamp burned brightly; two children appeared from another room; 'Mother who has Merlin brought home?'

'A little lost soul; now back to bed with you.'

'Her feet need bathing Jesse; they will bleed all over your bedspread.'

'First things first; come my dear drink this broth you need some good warm food; why, you are nothing but skin and bone; worry not about the bedspread it can be washed.'

The hot liquid burnt my throat but it was the best food I had had in ages.

'Take her to the chair by the fire Merlin while I fetch a bowl.'

He gently lifted me up and carried me to the chair; how I longed to stay nestled in his strong arms.

'The poor lass has no soles left on her shoes no wonder her feet are bleeding.' The woman knelt down and gently bathed my feet; at first they hurt even more but soon the pain eased. She then dried them carefully and put on some soothing balm. Merlin stood close by watching over me; until she said 'off with you Merlin go and help Zac in the stable; I need to get the lass out of her clothes and into a night shift.'

I nestled down under the patchwork quilt; I so loved the comfort of the feather bed and soon I felt a warm glow come over me and also a feeling of contentment. How long I slept I do not know but I awoke in a bath of perspiration and a horrible pain in my head that made me cry out. 'What bothers thee?' Jesse asked.

'I have a pain in my head and I am so hot.' I cried.

'My, my you are on fire;' she tried to get me to drink some cold water but I felt to weak and lay back down exhausted now all I wanted to do was sleep. 'Merlin' I called but it must have been just a whisper as Jesse did not respond.

I could smell his body odour and I felt the roughness of his coat against my face; I was safe again.

'She can't stay here Jesse she has a fever and until we know what is wrong you must think of yourself and your unborn baby and the children. Zac can drive me back home and then go on to Newquay and pick up my sister as she will know what ails the child; I am supposed to be setting sail the day after.'

I could hear his words but didn't have the energy to open my eyes; he called me a child didn't he realize I was a young woman; I didn't want him to leave I wanted him to stay with me for-ever I had never felt so safe as when I was in his arms. Was it the fever that burned through my body or the pain in my head that made me elucidate? I had called out to him and again he had come and saved me; he really must be Merlin the Magician or how else would he have known that I wanted him?

How long had I slept? I awoke to see the sun shining in on me and I was lying in a large bed just like the one mother and father used to sleep in; then I noticed the wallpaper it appeared like shining gold as the sun cast its light upon it; the gold was the colour of the trellis and climbing the trellis were large red roses. For a moment I gazed in amazement at my surroundings if this was Merlin's home he must be very rich and then my eyes filled with tears as I thought of him sharing the bed on which I lay with his wife; for surely he must have a wife.

'Good morning Vi you have had us so worried; I must go and tell Merlin that you are awake.'

Was that plump, pretty little woman Merlin's wife? I had noticed though that she had the same red hair as

Merlin; then I remembered that I had heard him saying he would send Zac for his sister.

'Good morning my Lady of the Lake it is so good to see you looking so much better.'

'How long have I been sick?'

'Almost a week; the doctor has been out to see you every day as you have been very poorly; he said that between the neglect, at the hands of your employer, and your perilous journey on foot all those miles it isn't much wonder that you ended up with pneumonia.'

'I thought I heard you say you were sailing on the morrow?'

'I couldn't leave until I knew you were well. As soon as the doctor says that you are fit to travel we will go back to my sister Elaine's home and then once you are settled in I must make plans to leave.'

I wanted to cry out that I didn't want him to leave; had he cast a spell over me I felt hypnotized by his very being; I longed for him to pick me up in his arms; I wanted to nestle close to him and feel his strong arms around me. He was magic; he had read my mind. He leaned over the bed and picked me up in his arms; he was so strong it was if I was a baby in his arms.

'Elaine said it would give you more pleasure if you lay on the sofa under the window and then you could see across the garden.' He gently put me down and wrapped a rug around my legs.

'I love the garden it is so pretty. Will you live here when you come back from your voyage?'

'I will be gone for many months this time so I have sold the house as it is too much for Jesse to look after with a new baby due any day.'

'Where will Jesse and Zac go?'

'They have been with me for many a year so I have given them their cottage and a few acres of land; they are sad to see me leave but obviously pleased to now own their own place and not have to answer to the new owner.'

'Why do you have to leave?'

'I have a contract to take our Cornish tin to lands far across the seven seas and sometimes I also take passengers as many are looking to better their lives in other countries.. I must leave now as I have work to oversee upon the ship so I will see you at supper and I do hope the doctor will leave me a good report.' He leaned over and kissed me gently on the brow; 'it is good to see the roses coming back into your beautiful face my little one.'

Within days my life changed completely; he took me to his sister's guest house; I felt completely at ease with her; the only thing that showed that they were siblings was her shock of flaming red hair; other than that she was small in stature where Merlin was quite tall and her waist line seemed to match her height. Elaine had already prepared an attic room for me as she kept the other rooms for her visiting guests. The delightful attic room had lace curtains draped on the two small windows and the most comfortable of single beds that had upon it a beautiful crocheted throw there was a small dressing table with a delft ware jug and basin and soap dish and one cane chair with a heavier crocheted patchwork rug and on the wooden floor boards there was a hand-made rag mat of pretty blue and cream pieces of cloth. I placed on a little bed-side table the photo of myself with my parents; how glad that through all the trials of the last weeks it had survived. What most impressed me was the view from the small attic windows as I could gaze out upon the azure waters and watch the fishing boats and larger vessels anchoring in the harbour. How I longed to get down to the shore line and sit in the warm summer sun.

Merlin had told me that when I was fully recovered I would be expected to assist Elaine with the running of the guest house. This I thought would be such a delight to help this lovely lady; I guessed that she might be a little older than her brother and put her age at about thirty.

I cried myself to sleep the night after Merlin had set sail on the afternoon tide. He had given me a big hug and kissed me lightly on the cheek. 'I will return' he had said but hadn't said 'when'. His sister later told me that sometimes Merlin was gone for two or more years. How could I possibly live with his sister and not daily think of him. It had been a new experience for me feeling a tingle through my very being when he had held me in his arms; if only for a fleeting moment. Was this longing I felt for him telling me that I had fallen in love with this wonderful man?

I must admit I was happy living with Elaine; she treated me as a younger sibling and although I made beds and washed and cleaned no chore was too difficult or too strenuous and also she would send me out shopping on an afternoon and when the weather was good she would tell me to take a walk and enjoy the fresh air that would put roses back in my pallid cheeks.

Once I was fully recovered I enjoyed walking along the cliff tops even on a stormy day. The bracing sea air brought Merlin closer to me as I thought of him standing at the helm of his ship and guiding his vessel over the monstrous waves. I prayed every night for his safe return.

As I stood and watched the high waves and white seahorses what really caught my imagination was the blow hole in the cliffs at Trevelgue Head; the old folk told tales that Bronze Age man had lived in the area and my imagination would run wild that they might have stood where I was standing and watched the stormy seas.

I would sit on the harbour wall and watch the fishing boats returning with their catch of herrings and pilchards and the big ships returning with their cargo of rocks that were turned into quick-lime in the lime kilns in the harbour.

Every-where was a hive of activity; walking down South Quay Hill I would watch the large schooners being built. Coal, limestone, timber and grain were brought in by ships and as I sat and watched I would look far out to sea and hoped and longed for the day when I would spy Merlin's ship on the horizon.

Weeks turned into months and months into years. Elaine had received long over-due letters; he had asked Elaine to give me his best wishes and he hoped that I was well and happy.

Each Sunday come rain or shine Elaine and I would walk to the Chapel of Ease in Bank Street; dedicated to St. Michael. It was very 'new' as Elaine would say and all the work of Rev. Nicholas Chudleigh who had laid the foundation stone in 1858 and the new church had opened the very same year in the September. Dressed in my Sunday best, bought with money left by Merlin for my up-keep, I felt really pretty something that I hadn't felt since those days in the big house with mamma and papa. I had many admiring glances and I know a few young farmers and lads that worked in the harbour had asked

Elaine for permission to 'court me'. Looking back I think that Elaine must have wondered why as some were very eligible young men but I knew where my feeling lay; but were these feeling just for the man who saved my life or did they go far deeper? I have already told you I had no knowledge of the 'love' of a man and a woman but one thing I did know that with each ship that came into the harbour and none were Merlin's I felt that my heart was breaking in two.

The second Christmas came and went and still no word of Merlin's return. The little guest house only had one guest so there was very little work for me to do. I found in the New Year that this guest and Elaine had become very close; so each afternoon I would wrap up warm against the elements and take myself off across the cliff tops. Passing along the way the little row of white houses and the coastguard station that had been built in 1825. I would often spend time chatting to the 'old sea-salt' in the Watch House; he would tell me tales of smugglers who left their haul in the Tea Caverns under the cliffs at Gazzle and how a hundred horses would be waiting on Crantock Beach even on the Sabbath to pick up the contraband. When I asked him why he sat there looking out to sea he said it was his job to still watch for smugglers; ship wrecks and any invading forces. He also watched for the sighting of shoals of pilchards and then the little boats would go out and let down their nets; a big business in Newquay. Storms brought out the lifeboat that was launched off Towan Beach and what a task that was for man and beast as it was brought down on a carriage pulled by horses and hauled off by men in order to save lives. Every ship-wreck brought tears to my eyes and a pain in my heart; where was Merlin? When would he return? The silver frame now held a photo of the man that I held so close to my heart; I had found it in the drawer in my attic room and as Elaine never ventured up the steep stairs to the attic my secret was safe. Dare I tell you that each night after I had knelt and said my prayers I placed a kiss upon his face; 'May God protect you and bring you home to me.' It never entered my head; well, if it did I soon cast such thoughts aside, that he might have a wife and family in some distant land and would never return.

March came in like a lion but the blustery winds did not deter my walks along the headline. Easter that year came early and after Church on Easter Sunday Elaine took my arm as we walked back home. 'Be happy for me Vi; Thomas has asked me to marry him.' She took her glove off her left hand and there sparking on her third finger was a diamond ring. I didn't care who was watching as I put my arms around her and gave her a kiss; 'I guessed you were more than 'just good friends' as you so often told me; I wish you all the happiness in the world.'

'I had a letter from Merlin; he was leaving the New World at the end of April and hopefully he will be home by June when we plan to marry. He also sends his best wishes to you and asked were you being courted. I will still 'run' my little guest house; the little attic room is yours for as long as you wish as you are such a great help to me.'

From the middle of May I spent hours sitting on the headland watching the schooners and large ships enter the harbour. Elaine had had no further letters from Merlin but her hopes were high and the bans were called in the

Church and plans were made for the wedding to take place on the longest day; the summer solstice. There was a magical feeling in the air that made me think more and more about Merlin and how he had seemed to have appeared from no-where when he saved me from death's door. If I closed my eyes and called his name would he hear me? Would when I opened my eyes see his ship on the horizon. It was such a beautiful evening; the sky was cloudless and the sun, like a ball of fire, was setting in the west. I lay on my back in the heather and gazed up to heaven; the stars were just beginning to peep. 'I really must be getting home' I thought, 'Elaine will be worrying about me.' Still I lingered; one star shone brighter than all the others; words that I had read on a postcard came to mind. 'Star light, star bright; the first star I see tonight; I wish I may, I wish I might; Have the wish I wish tonight. I wish,' I started to say aloud but hesitated; what if someone heard me; sitting up I looked around but there was no-one in sight; again I said 'I wish, I wish for Merlin to sail into the harbour; please star shining bright grant my wish tonight. Merlin, Merlin come home to me;' I called his name and hoped that it would be carried on the breeze. Dusk was falling quickly so I got to my feet and hurried back along the cliff path and down South Quay Hill. Elaine would certainly be cross as she always told me to be home before dusk. I over-heard a few old men talking as they sat on the harbour wall; 'rather late for a ship that size to come into the harbour; the captain will have to dock at sea and use the small boat to come ashore.'

'I can't believe my eyes,' said the other, 'it is Davies the Red's ship.'

As soon as I heard his name I stifled a scream of delight; my wish had come true; there was most certainly magic in the air. I ran down to the shore and as soon as Merlin stepped from the small boat I ran into his arms.

'My! My! Little lady I never expected such a welcome.'

I didn't care that the tide was ebbing and flowing over by feet and my shoes were getting wet. Next thing Merlin had picked me up and carried me to the harbour wall. 'Welcome home Davies; what cargo have you brought us this time?'

'A water nymph I found on the sea-shore.' He jested and he put me down right by the two old men.

Taking my hand he said; 'We'd better hurry my Lady of the Lake or Elaine will be taking the rolling pin to us.'

As we entered the cottage I noticed that no longer was Merlin's hair and beard the flaming red that it had been when he sailed away almost two years ago it was now more grey and as the candle-light shone on his face it gave him even a more mystical look. In fact, I liked his appearance even more and my heart was all of a flutter. I whispered to him; 'did you hear me calling you?'

'Many, many times,' he replied.

It was great to have Merlin home but I was rather disappointed that he paid very little attention to me. He spent time working on his ship and on a few occasions had travelled to distant towns on business.

Preparations were made for the wedding that Elaine had said would just be a quiet event. Merlin was to 'give her away' and I was to be her attendant. She looked so pretty in her white lace gown and veil and I felt so grown up in the dress she had chosen for me of pale blue silk.

'It matches your eyes,' said Merlin; 'you really do look like my Lady of the Lake.'

They were the first kind words he had spoken to me since his arrival and made me blush.

After the wedding we had lunch, in what to me was a 'posh' hotel and then waved the happy couple off on the train that was to take them to Bath; an exciting experience as the train had not long arrived in Newquay. Merlin had arranged everything for the happy couple.

A cloud suddenly loomed over me when I realized I would be alone in the guest house as Elaine had cancelled all boarders for the month of June. Merlin had spent a great deal of time on board his ship and had not stayed in the guest house as visits to other towns had also taken him away from Newquay.

'I've hired a horse and trap as I thought you might like a trip to Tintagel; I believe you said you once lived nearby.'

'I'd love to,' I said, 'but I had better go and change my dress.'

'There is no need; you look so pretty wear it for me; it was just bought for the day.'

'Surely it will take too long it is over twenty miles.'

'I've arranged rooms for us in a local inn. I thought it would give you a chance to visit your mother's grave.'

One minute I felt elated the next at the thought of my mother I felt near to tears.

The scenery was pleasant as we travelled along the country roads and lanes; catching glimpses of the azure blue sea as the lanes twisted and turned. Our conversation was jovial but really it was about something or nothing; I learned nothing of his life as a seafarer. He told me he had been to the New World; and that it was a vast nation; its people of many races and creeds.

As we entered the gates to a large house memories came flooding back; surely this was the house where I was born; I saw the rolling lawns and the path that led down to a small bay; I closed my eyes and remembered as a small child playing on the sandy beach, I held back my tears but Merlin noticed and taking my hand he said; 'I'm sorry I made you cry little one perhaps it was rather thoughtless of me to bring you here; it is no longer the home you remember it has had many alterations as it is now a hotel.'

The front entrance was just as I remembered, as was the vast hall except for a small area that now housed a desk where it appeared that visitors registered.

'Your rooms are ready Mr. Davies said an elderly lady who was sitting behind the desk.

'Thank you Maud.'

'No luggage Sir,' said a young lad who was dressed in the uniform of a bell-boy.

'Not this time Joe, just a fleeting visit.'

Everyone seemed to know him and he appeared to call them all by their Christian names.

'Have you stayed here before?' I asked.

He laughed; 'I own it.'

As we entered what looked like a cage to me I felt it suddenly moving and when it stopped we were on another floor. Everything appeared to be newly decorated and the carpet below my feet felt so luxurious. Another bell-boy opened a door that led into a room and from the view at the window I recognized it as my parent's room but everything had changed; the wallpaper, the light fittings and the small anti-room that had been mother's dressing room was now a bathroom; what luxury.

'Rest a while and I will knock on your door when it is time for dinner which will be about seven o'clock.'

'Dinner', I thought, 'surely he meant supper.'

I slipped off my dress and my pretty slippers and ventured into the bathroom; what a surprise awaited me there were soft white towels and sweet scented soaps and pretty glass jars of bath salts. I had seen such pictures of these items in papers that had been left at the guest house but never thought I would ever wash in such fragrant soaps. Then I began to wonder if I was to stay the night in this room I had not brought a nightdress. Turning back the bedspread before lying upon the bed I found a pretty nightdress on the pillow; it reminded me of the pretty nightdresses mother had hand sewn for me when I was a child.

I was too excited to rest as so many thoughts were going through my mind. The main one being Merlin and why had he brought me here? If his thoughts were of seducing me he would not have arranged separate rooms. I must admit I was rather disappointed as from what I had read in books my body was sending out so many signals and I was ready for love. Then I thought of Elaine and recalled her saying that she had kept herself 'pure' until her wedding night. Had she been trying to tell me to remain a virgin until my wedding night? Why was I thinking such thoughts Merlin had only ever kissed me on the cheek in a brotherly fashion and never had he mentioned any words to show he had feelings other than brotherly ones for me?

I noticed from the ornate clock on the mantle-shelf that it was gone six o'clock surely I hadn't fallen asleep.

I quickly got up and tidied the bed; why had I bothered tis was now a hotel; I was afraid to venture into the big bath so just quickly washed my face and hands and put some cream from a pretty pot on my face; well the label did say 'face cream'; I noticed a brush and comb on a side table so undoing the bow that tied back my hair I quickly combed it through and re-tied the ribbon. Lastly, I slipped on my brides-maid dress and sprayed on some lavender scented perfume from a bottle standing on the same little table. The clock now said six forty five and I was ready and I must admit feeling rather excited of dining in what was now most luxurious surroundings.

I heard the awaited knock on the door to my room and eagerly rushed to open it.

'Viviane, my beautiful Lady of the Lake, may I escort you to dinner?' As he hooked his arm in mine a shiver ran down my spine. 'I think I had better warn you I have one more surprise for you.'

What could it possibly be? I felt quite excited, had he brought me here to propose to me? He led me towards a table by the window and as we approached a man, who had his back to us, rose from his chair and as he turned I gasped and as I felt Merlin's arms around me I fainted.

The smell of the smelling salts under my nose revived me and then I heard Merlin's words; 'Vi, my darling Viviane I am so sorry I didn't think I just thought it would be a lovely surprise for you as so often you have said that you wondered what had happened to your father. I met him a few weeks ago when visiting Bath to arrange a booking for Elaine's honeymoon and your father was managing the hotel. I asked him would he like to run my 'new' hotel and when I told him it was his old home he was delighted to accept. I have put him in full charge of the running of the hotel as I set sail for the Americas the day after tomorrow.

There was a mixture of sadness and joy in Merlin's words. Sadness that again he was leaving with no words to me that he would ever love me; yet had I heard him calling me 'darling'? There was also great joy in being reunited with my father; there was no denying that in the years we had been apart he had aged but to me at this moment in time he looked more like my beloved father than the last image that had remained with me of a drunken, broken man I had been taken from almost six years earlier.

Dinner was served by smartly dressed waiters and with the exception of a glass of wine I had had at Elaine's wedding breakfast I had never tasted wine before so it was new to my palate and I think made me feel rather merry; we had so much catching up to do and then Merlin dropped another surprise.

'Elaine and Thomas have decided to sell the guest house and I thought it would be nice for you to come and live here with your father; there will be no rush but when you are ready just let your father know.'

I slept very little that night; the moon shone brightly in through my window and the stars sparkled like myriads of diamonds. My wish had come true he had returned home but not to stay he was sailing far away again and out of my life. We only had one day left and he had promised to take me to Tintagel the legendary birthplace of King Arthur and where Merlin performed his magic on Uther Pendragon. How I wish that I, like Viviane of Arthurian legend, was able to perform 'magic' on Merlin and bewitch him into never leaving me.

I was sad at leaving my father but promised that within the month I would arrange to move to the hotel. Tears filled my eyes as I hugged and kissed him 'goodbye'.

I had tried to remove the creases from my dress but on putting it on I no longer felt like the princess I had felt the previous evening. I hadn't bothered to tie back my hair and as we drove along the coastal path my hair blew wild in the breeze.

'You are so beautiful,' he said as he brought the horse to a stand-still on the grass just a few yards from the ruins of Tintagel Castle. I was about to step down when his arms were around me as he lifted me down; for a moment he held me close; I lifted my face and looked into his dark brown eyes how I longed for him to kiss me but the moment was lost but what had I seen in his eyes? It appeared to be a deep sadness.

His mood changed as he stood on the rocky out-crop and after looking out to sea he turned and recited these words:

'I must go down to the seas again; to the lonely sea and the sky; and all I ask is a tall ship and a star to steer her by, and the wheel's kick and the wind's song and the white sails shaking; and a grey mist on the sea's face and a grey dawn breaking. I must go down to the sea again for the call of the running tide; is a wild call a clear call that may not be denied; and all I ask is a windy day and the white clouds flying, the flung spray and the blown spume and the sea-gulls crying. I must go down to the sea again to the vagrant gypsy life, to the gull's way and the whales way, where the wind like a whetted knife, and all I ask is a merry yarn from a laughing fellow rover,

and a quiet sleep and a sweet dream when the long trick is over.'

I applauded him but there were tears in my eyes as I felt it was his way of telling me that he had to go to sea as it was his way of life; the only way he knew.

'Did you write those words?' I asked

'No', he replied but there was a sadness upon his voice; a poet by the name of John Mansfield. 'My sweet Lady of the Lake do not shed tears over me. I want to love you but it will be no life for you to be left for months and perhaps even years as I sail the seven seas. Perhaps, I should have said that I do love you and I want to make love to you and hold you in my arms from sunset to sunrise but how can I make love to you and perhaps leave you with my seed within your womb and your good name lost to you forever.'

Together we walked back to where the horse and trap stood; no words were spoken between us; I for one didn't know what to say. I wanted to cry out 'I love you, I want you to make love to me and I don't care about my good name.'

We sat with our backs against the trap and unpacked the lunch that had been prepared for us but my appetite for food had left me and had been replaced with an appetite or perhaps I should say a yearning to feel his body next to mine. 'I have to sail on the morning tide my ship is already laden with a cargo.'

I wanted to hide my longing so I jokingly said, 'I suppose you have a woman in every port that satisfies your needs. You don't care how I feel about you and how those feelings have grown since our first meeting. I can still smell that same body odour I smelt when you put your coat over me in the trap and when you picked me up in your arms. Don't you care that I too have feelings and that I love you and long for you. Can't you take me to sea with you?'

As if my words had hit him like a thunder bolt his arms were around me and his lips were upon mine; no longer was it a brotherly kiss it was what I had been waiting for. 'No my Lady of the Lake I do not have a woman in every port I have had you on my mind and close to my heart from that very first day I found a poor little lass drowning in the mire.' We lay together in the long grass and his kisses grew more passionate and then he pulled away from me for just a moment as he undid the buttons on the front of my dress; how can I describe the feelings of an innocent virgin as he fondled my breasts that tingled with his every caress. He lifted the skirt of my dress and as I felt his fingers touch those secret places known only to me I moaned with pleasure; between his kisses and his caresses I knew that my body yearned for the final act and realized that even in my ignorance of love making I knew that he too was ready to enter me as his manhood was hard against me. 'I love you,' he said as he started to undo the belt of his trousers, 'I want you my darling Viviane.'

It was not to be for as he raised my dress and lay upon me the horse moved towards us and would have trampled over us if we hadn't quickly moved. The moment was lost as was his erection. We laughed it off but then he turned to me and said; 'perhaps it was for the good.'

We travelled back to Newquay in silence; I wanted to put out my hand and touch him I wanted him to want me; to stop the trap and make love in the back where once I had lay with his coat over me. I knew he was aware of my feelings. As the evening brought a sudden chill I shivered and as if reading my previous thoughts he stopped the trap but not to take me into the back to make love but to take off his coat and put it over my shoulders.

He reined in the horse outside the guest house and getting down he opened the door; I made no attempt to get down as I wanted just one more time to feel his arms around me surely then the longing would return and he would carry me into the house and to bed where we would make passionate love until the morning. Before returning he lit a candle in the hall. 'Are you staying there all night?' he teased. He came around to my side and lifted me down and for a fleeting moment he held me close but there the closeness ended. He did not carry me into the house or even to the doorway. 'Do not come down to the harbour to see me off I shall be gone before you awake. My little Lady of the Lake find someone to love you as you should be loved.'

'I will never stop loving you and no-one else will ever take your place.'

'Never is a long time.' He said and before leaving he kissed me longingly on the lips. 'I do love you and always will. Goodbye sweet Viviane.'

I was tired and heart-broken and longed to sleep but as dawn broke I stood at the window and watched him sail away into the distant horizon. 'Merlin, Merlin,' I cried, 'come back to me.'

It would be two days before Elaine and Thomas would be returning. Would things have been better for me if I could have 'cried' on Elaine's shoulder? There was nothing for me to do in the home; everything was neat and tidy. I decided I would do some shopping on the day of their return so feeling so depressed after watching Merlin's boat disappear into the far horizon I got back into bed and burying my face in the pillow I cried and cried and felt as though my heart was broken in two; well as far as I as concerned it was. I felt it was pointless to get up so there I stayed all day and as dusk fell I stood by the window and gazed out to sea and again I called his name 'Merlin come back to me; I want you and I need you; I love you Merlin.' The thought of him and the picture of him on my bedside table started me crying; it wasn't worth me living without him; why, oh! Why had he saved my life only to end up breaking my heart?

If I was to go and live with my father I may as well go as soon as Elaine and Thomas returned. They wouldn't want me 'playing gooseberry'. Unable to sleep I took down a wicker case from on top of the wardrobe; I had examined it when I first had come to live with Elaine and knew it was empty I decided to pack my clothes and the few possession I had accumulated. Because of the generosity of Merlin in supporting me I now had quite an array of clothes. Then I thought, perhaps I should leave them behind as I had arrived with nothing so should I leave with nothing? On the top of the case I placed Merlin's picture in the silver frame. I had an urge to remove it as it really wasn't mine and just leave the picture of my mother and father and myself taken in those happy childhood days. My thoughts were in turmoil; why had Merlin bought my old home: why had he installed my father as maître d'hôtel? He must have cared a great deal about me to have done that; yet not enough to leave the sea and marry me.

I was hungry but I couldn't bother to eat breakfast so picking up the shopping basket and taking some money from the old tea caddy I made an early start to the shops. I would prepare them a lovely meal and then send a message to father to come and pick me up. I really hadn't considered everything as my only thought was getting away from Newquay and by doing so I would not see the ocean going vessel in the harbour and therefore, close my mind to Merlin. If I had thought it through I would have realized that living in my old home, although, it had changed greatly it was still full of memories and from every window in the front of the great house one could gaze out upon the sea and in doing so Merlin would remain close.

By early afternoon I had prepared everything and leaving a note to welcome them home I decided to take a walk across the cliff tops to clear my mind of all my silly thoughts. It had been a beautiful morning but within an hour after leaving home the weather changed. I recalled what the 'old salts' would say; 'sea mist coming down so quickly means that a storm was brewing.' Why did everything remind me of Merlin? Even down to the sea mist on that treacherous day when I lost my way. I really must turn back or surely I would get lost or even the worse could happen if I came too close to the cliff top. There were unusual noises echoing on the air; a rustle as of an animal walking over the heather; a loose rock rolling down the hilly surround; was it the sound of a horse's breath that echoed in my ears. I began to feel frightened as one didn't live in such a community without hearing tales of ghosts and the 'ancients' who lived here centuries before. Were the dead that were buried on top of the cliffs rising to haunt me? I began to feel icy cold and as I shivered goose-bumps crept down my arms and down my spine; then the hairs on the back of my neck began to stand on end and when a hand grasped me on the shoulder as if to push me to the ground I screamed and called; 'Merlin help me'.

'Not this time you whoring bitch he is far out at sea.'

The voice sounded familiar but before I could utter another word his hand was across my mouth and he pushed me to the ground. 'I've been following you for weeks and now I can get my reward you escaped me once before but this time there is no-one to save you. I would have liked to have been the one to have 'broken you in' but Davies had the pleasure of doing that.'

It was then I realized that my attacker was the horrid Shaun Murphy.

The sea mist had become quite dense but I could see the man who now had his foot upon my belly. I tried to move but as I did so he pressed his foot down hard upon me. I could see in the dim light he was undoing the buttons on his trousers; he moved his foot but before I had chance to move he was on top of me. He pressed his mouth hard against my lips and because I made no response he bit deep into my lips.

As his hands tried to reach beneath my clothes I tensed my leg muscles and held my knees together.

'Open your legs you bitch I'm ready for you.' He shouted obscenities at me; 'I'll take you one way or another; how would you like me to cut your throat. He pulled open my blouse and grabbed my breast. I had to stop him, he was hurting me but as I moved he forced my legs apart.

'Merlin, Merlin;' I screamed. I felt him hard against me but then as if a gale force wind had suddenly blown up he was torn from me; I was free. I rolled over and tried to get up but every bone in my body was hurting. Then I heard a gun being fired and a horrendous scream and then there was silence. Who had fired the shot? Had anyone been killed? I tried again to get to my feet and then I felt myself being lifted up.

'My darling, my sweet little Lady of the Lake I was a fool to leave you.'

'Merlin,' was all I could say before I fainted.

I awoke in my bed with Elaine fussing over me, bathing my lips and putting a herbal balm upon my painful breast.

'Merlin' I said 'He is a magician he heard my calls and came to my rescue.'

'I like that thought,' said Elaine 'but it didn't quite happen that way. He had trouble with the engine it wasn't getting up enough steam and decided to return to harbour. He came looking for you and saw the note you had left for me and decided to go and meet you. All I can say is thank God that he did.'

'I heard a gun-shot what happened to Murphy?'

'Merlin fired and hit Murphy but had no intention of killing him but Murphy turned on Merlin and a fight broke out and during that fight Murphy lost his footing and went over the cliff-top. When the tide turns his body will soon be found and the crime of murder will be put on Merlin as he was seen walking along the cliff path. His engine has been repaired and he is ready to leave.'

'No! No!' I cried, 'he cannot leave without me.'

'He has no intention of leaving without you. He has paid a lad to take your box down to the harbour and now that you are awake and I have done all I can you too must leave because by noon the police will be looking for you as well as Merlin as you are aware you spoke to people as you left the town and headed up the path to the headland. God go with you Viviane and protect you and Merlin from all harm one day I am sure we will meet again.' She hugged me and kissed me and with Thomas by my side I made my way to the harbour. I was still trembling after my ordeal but now I began to shiver as thoughts raced through my head; what would happen to us if we were caught? Surely Merlin, if found guilty, would be hung or even if there was no case against him the possibility was high that he would be sent to Botany Bay even if the death was an accident.

I was helped aboard a small boat and as the boat was rowed from the shoreline I looked back and could see just a flicker of a candle in my attic room. I remembered Elaine's words; 'I will keep a candle burning for you to light your way back home.' As we came alongside the ship I looked up and saw Merlin holding a lantern and at the same time I noticed the rope ladder. Was I expected to climb that? I was guided by a young sailor and slowly I made my way to the top; exhausted I collapsed into Merlin's arms.

'Hush, hush my darling don't cry I promise everything will be all right.' His cabin below deck was far better than ever I had anticipated. 'Make yourself 'at home'', he said as he put me down on his bunk bed.

'Where will you sleep?' I questioned.

'I can string up a hammock on the bridge.'

'Don't leave me I am so frightened.'

'There is no need to be afraid you are safe now. I have to leave you for just a short while until we are safely out into the Atlantic. You are still trembling my love; I will send old Walter with something to warm you; I promise I will be back as soon as possible.' He kissed me on the cheek and lightly touching my swollen lips he said; 'no-one will ever hurt you again my sweet Viviane.'

I lay upon the bunk fully dressed; old Walter brought me a steaming bowl of what appeared to be some form of soup and the young sailor, a mere lad of no more years than thirteen, brought my wicker case. I was too tired and now my body and sore legs seemed to hurt even more. I must have fallen asleep but something had disturbed me; I opened my eyes and found Merlin lying by my side and he was gently smoothing my hair.

'Merlin,' I said, 'my body hurts so much.'

'Why don't you undress and put on your night shift the soft material will help to soothe your tender body.'

'I haven't the energy and the pain is so bad.'

He rose from my side and gently helping me to sit up he removed my coat and then my blouse and skirt. 'Elaine has given me some balm to soothe your sore body are you able to apply it or shall I?'

My arms were covered in bruises and every movement made me want to cry but how could I let a man apply balm to my breasts and stomach and to the bruises on my inner thighs?

I watched as he poured some solution into a bowl and then he came and sat by my side and so very gently bathed my sore and still bleeding lips. 'How I wish I could kiss them better.'

His gentle touch was to me, at that time, like a butterfly kiss. Putting the bowl down he did not ask again but undid the ribbons on my bodice and very gently slipped it off my shoulders; I felt my colour rise as I realized I was almost naked; a silly thought came into my head I wondered how he would have managed to undo all the hooks if I had been wearing stays. As he rubbed the balm in my breasts it was as if by magic he had taken away the pain; after the horrific experience I had had only hours before how could I now have a longing in my groins for Merlin to make love to me. My thoughts, or was it Merlin's touch made my nipples harden; I wanted him so much I lay motionless as he pushed down my bloomers to rub the soothing cream on the bruises on my stomach where that beast had trod upon me.

'Damn the bastard may he rot in hell.' Merlin said as he moved away to put down the almost empty jar.

The only bruises left that hadn't had the soothing balm were the ones on my thighs. I recalled that Elaine had said they were the most painful.

I panicked when I saw him undoing the straps of my case as I knew that on the top he would see his photograph.

'I know very little about lady's attire so can I assume that this is your night shift; I think I can see here some of my sister's fine needlework.'

Was he just making conversation to cover his embarrassment? I too was beginning to feel embarrassed as it had been hours since I had relieved myself; how was I to ask him where could I go? I must have blushed crimson as I asked; 'where can I go to pass water?'

'There are facilities behind the screen.' He helped me to get to my feet and before he had a chance to slip my nightdress over my head my bloomers dropped round my ankles. I sat back down to remove them but as I went to lift my leg I cried out in pain.

The oaths that he uttered on seeing the bruises I cannot repeat. He lifted my legs back onto the bed and forgotten was my need to use the facilities behind the screen as every touch of his hand took away the pain but it brought on a new pain, a throbbing and a longing more intense than when we almost made love at Tintagel.

'I love you,' I whispered.

'I love you too my beautiful maiden. I want you now but how can I make love to you I do not wish to cause you more anguish. I will lie with you until you fall asleep and dream my Lady of the Lake my sweet Viviane of the time when I will make you mine.'

He helped me to my feet as nature called and when I very slowly and very painfully returned to the bunk I found he had removed his clothes; I gazed in wonderment at his fine physique; and could not turn my eyes away from his erect manhood. Why does one have stupid thoughts at such momentous moments? I could not but wonder how it could possibly penetrate me? For a moment he held me close then turning back the rug he lay me down and then lying next to me he began to caress my body. I wanted to put my hand out and touch him but although his caresses, at first, excited me soon I began to feel drowsy; the warmth of his body next to mine was a comfort.

'Sleep my little one, sleep.'

Sleep I did; not just until daybreak but well into the afternoon, I awoke to see the sun streaming in through the porthole and I then I saw Merlin sitting by a desk on which were rolled up papers and many nautical instruments.

'Merlin,' I called, 'I thought I had dreamt it all but it is real I am at sea with you.'

I cannot recall how many days passed before I felt strong enough to get dressed; I lay upon the bunk in my nightdress conscious of the fact that beneath it I was naked. Old Walter brought me food; a form of gruel for my breakfast and it seemed that all he could cook was soup or stew. Merlin worked in the cabin he told me that he was plotting the ship's course and all the many instruments helped him and he also kept a daily log of all activities on board the ship. I don't know if he was afraid of the consequences but he spent no further nights with me.

He walked with me on deck; showed me the big boiler room and the stack of coal that fed the big gaping and ever hungry mouth of the boiler. He stood behind me and held my hands as he let me turn the ship's wheel. My bruises were now turning purple and as my lips healed they began to crack with the salt air old Walter gave me some cooking lard to grease my lips. How glad I was that there were no gale force winds and no rough seas. I chatted with the crew and heard many tales of their adventures on the Seven Seas. How they had all nearly lost their lives rounding the Cape; how pirates had fired at them in the South Seas. The 'cargo' they hated carrying were the prisoners bound for Botany Bay. I shivered at the thought that this very ship could have been taking my beloved in chains to Botany Bay.

'Ten of the Best'

I had not counted the days as time had been lost to me at the beginning of the voyage but surely it had been more than three weeks since we had left Newquay. One morning I was awakened with a kiss from Merlin.

'Put on your pretty blue dress today and pretty yourself up as today is going to be special.'

Before I had time to ask 'why' he had left. I gazed out of the port-hole and could see a flock of gulls diving into the sea and flying high overhead. I wondered were we reaching land and was that the reason why Merlin wanted me to dress in my best.

Another surprise awaited me when Merlin returned to the cabin in his best naval uniform. 'We are about to dock in Boston Harbour a good friend of mine will be waiting for us.'

As I stepped up on deck I hadn't been aware that a day could possibly be so hot. The ship had already docked and below on the quay stood a great number of people. So this was New England; I was awe struck not just by the people but by the number of ships in the dock. I had always assumed that the ship Merlin sailed was his but it was only when I saw him in his fine uniform that he told me he was a captain in Queen Victoria's navy. There was so little I knew about the man who I loved so deeply. I waited on deck with Merlin who stood by my side with his arm around my waist holding me close.

'Permission to come aboard.'

'Permission granted.'

I saw a man in naval uniform sporting a finer set of whiskers than Merlin and following him on board an elegant mature lady dressed in fine silks and wearing a huge hat and carrying a parasol to protect her fair complexion from the strong rays of the sun.

'Viviane may I introduce you to Admiral and Mrs. Edward Stevenson.'

I didn't know if I should take the Admiral's outstretched hand or curtsy to his wife. I had never met such important people.

The admiral's wife must have noticed that I was ill at ease as taking my hand she said; 'Let us go below deck out of this heat.'

A young girl, whom I hadn't noticed, followed us. She seemed to be struggling to carry numerous boxes and on arriving back in Merlin's cabin all was revealed.

'What is happening today Mrs. Stevenson? I thought we were disembarking.'

'Please do call me Rose. I expect the men are having a tot of rum I think Merlin will need it I don't carry out his plans. He has left it to me to tell you that today is to be your wedding day.'

I just stared at her in utter disbelief; and all I could mutter was 'how?'

'I offered to buy you a bridal gown but Merlin insisted you had a dress that he wished for you to wear; he suggested that I bought a blue bonnet as blue as the lake by our home and pretty velvet slippers. My girl will dress your hair and perhaps add a little colour to your sallow cheeks. All Merlin has told us is that you have been through difficult times.'

'Surely he couldn't have sent all this in a message?'

'While you slept the ship docked and Merlin came ashore and spent the night with us.'

'How can we marry; the bans haven't been called and we are not American citizens.'

'You will marry on board this ship that is classed as English soil and my husband as a naval officer has the right to perform the ceremony. Come let us prepare you for your special day.'

My hair was brushed until it shone and tied back with a deep blue velvet bow. When it came time to slip on my own blue dress that I had worn to Elaine's wedding Rose muffled a cry of disbelief as my body was still covered with the fading bruises. The 'bonnet' was trimmed with lace and two ribbons hung loosely from the corners. I had tried to tie them but was told it was the fashion to let them just hang loosely. My slippers were also of deep blue velvet. I asked how had she known the right size and was told that Merlin had taken one of my slippers with him. Another large box revealed a posy of white roses tied together with the same deep blue velvet ribbon. All this had been bought this very morning.

'Come,' said Rose; 'your bridegroom awaits.'

As we walked across the deck the young girl held over me a parasol in the deepest of blue embossed with white roses.

Merlin was standing on the bridge and as I joined him his eyes lit up; and I heard his whisper; 'My Lady of the Lake.'

The only words I heard were Merlin saying 'I do' and my shy response as I promised to 'love, honour and obey him.' Then the final words; 'I now pronounce you husband and wife; you may kiss your bride.'

As we disembarked the crew showered us with rice and made an arch with their rifles for us to pass under. We dined in a very posh hotel and I assumed that it would be here that we would spend our wedding night but to my surprise as dusk began to fall over the harbour

Merlin took me back to the ship. We were 'piped' aboard and cheers resounded across the deck. I learned that most of the crew had been given shore leave with only a skeleton crew left on board.

Merlin picked me up and carried me as he said 'over the threshold' into his cabin. Edward had arranged for champagne to be left on ice for us and Rose that the cabin was to be bedecked with flowers. I was in seventh heaven. I was now married to the most mysterious and magical man in the whole world and as far as I was concerned the most handsome.

He stood for a moment and held me at arms-length; 'do you know my darling that from the moment I first picked you up and carried you to my trap you cast a spell over me; I realized then that one day I would make you mine.'

'I too have kept a memory close to me; it was the smell of your body odour mixed with your pipe tobacco that remained with me and you still have that special odour. There are still questions I ask myself and have no answer and I suppose there is a rational reason but from that very first time you saved my life I have believed that you have magical powers as when in times of trouble or great longing I have called your name you have as if by magic answered my call.'

'Call me now my darling if you have a great yearning for your lover; call me and I will come to you.'

'Sit by your desk and close your eyes and when I call come to me.'

'You play games with me; two can play at these games.'

I went behind the screen and quickly without any coyness removed all my clothes. Rose had given me some perfume and this I sprayed on my body. The thought of making love set my body on fire and my firm young breasts tingled with anticipation.

Before I moved from behind the screen I called; 'Merlin, Merlin my lover where are you?' As I stepped into the room I saw him waiting for me and into his arms I ran both of us as naked as the day we were born. His lips were hungry for mine and picking me up he carried me to the bunk; his foreplay excited me and brought me to fever pitch time and time again; I wound my legs around him and pulling him close I was ready for him; I cried out like the gulls flying around the ship but my question had been answered everything was made for a purpose and nothing was impossible.

We slept in each other's arms; we woke and drank champagne and made love until the sun shone in on us through the port-hole and then slept until noon.

'I have one more surprise for you my beautiful Lady of the Lake; today I will take you home.'

'How can we return to England?'

'Not to England my love but to the town of Plymouth in New England.'

It was the home I could never have imagined living in. Merlin took no more long voyages but had received instructions from England and took monthly tours around the coast of Canada. I was the perfect wife and Merlin the perfect lover. Our lovemaking intensified and there were no limits to how we found new ways to please each other. The following year we took a holiday away from the heat of the towns and journeyed up into the mountains. The small house we had rented beside a mountain lake was idyllic. We swam in the pure, clear cold water and made love in the long grass. We climbed to the top of the mountain and like two children we called out to Elaine our voices resounded from hill top to hill top. 'Do you think she has heard us?' I asked.

By the fall my wish that I had made one starry night by the moonlit lakeside had come true I was carrying Merlin's child.

Letters from home arrived frequently and Merlin was pleased to learn that the death of Shaun Murphy had been put down to accidental. That in a drunken stupor he had fallen from the cliff-top. No mention was made of a bullet wound. 'I don't understand that,' said Merlin 'I must have missed.'

Merlin, Viviane, and Elaine all part of the Arthurian legend so what else could we but call our son born the following May but Arthur. Merlin had instructions to return home so in the November we closed up our home and set sail for the Old Country. I already had a Christmas present for Merlin. The voyage was far from calm and the stormy weather and treacherous seas made me feel so sea sick. I spent most of the time in the cabin only going on deck when Merlin shouted Newquay ahead. It was early morning and from the deck I could see the light of a candle burning in the attic room. Elaine had wrote and told us that as the tourists were swarming into Newquay by train they had decided to keep the guest house.

We spent a wonderful Christmas but Merlin couldn't understand why, even on shore, I was still being sick every morning. I put him out of his misery on Christmas morning by telling him that by the summer Arthur would have a baby brother or sister. New Year was spent with father in the hotel; Elaine and Thomas joined us. Leaving Arthur with Elaine we wrapped up warm against the winter chill and took the trap to Tintagel.

'Shall we make love in the grass,' teased Merlin. If it had been springtime my answer would have been 'yes'.

We held hands as we gazed out to sea. 'One day said Merlin we will set sail again and return to the New World but for now our home is here in England's green and pleasant land.'

I know how much he loved the sea, it was in his blood, his new post was on the south coast and at the end of the month we were again picking up our roots and moving, quite ironically to Plymouth.

He kissed me passionately as we stood in the magical surroundings of Tintagel. We were lost in time he was Merlin the magician and I his Lady Viviane. We had cast a spell upon each other a spell that would bind us together for eternity.

The End

First published in 2014 in 'Mammy Val's Little Book of Allsorts'

Heaven on Earth

I switched the radio on hoping that there would be some music that I could sing along with as I did my daily chores but what I heard really scared me.

'The Met. Office has issued a warning that a large meteor is expected to fall causing devastating damage; some religious leaders have stated that the end of the world is nigh.' I switched off the radio I didn't wish to hear this scaremongering talk.

'Come on boy let's go 'walkies'. It was a beautiful autumn day; quite warm for October and the sun's rays enhanced the autumnal colours of the trees in the wood. We left behind the woodland and followed the mountain stream up into the hills. How I wish, like the dog, to be able to paddle in the babbling brook. I stopped and listened the air was full of music; the wind rustling through the trees; the birds singing their tuneful lilt and then the sound of the brook as it journeyed on to far-away places. This was a piece of heaven on earth. This was a favourite walk of Bruno as he loved to run through the ferns and hide from me and then spring out as I approached. Up and up we journeyed; now the air was far more bracing and the wind caught my breath but it was worth the effort as finally we reached the crest of the mountain; exhausted I sat on one of the big boulders that surrounded what must have been an animal's lair or ancient burial place; Bruno sprawled out by my side he too had over-exerted himself but it had been worth the effort as I looked down on the beautiful valley and far in the distance the azure blue sea. God was in his heaven and all was right with the world. How true were those beautiful words all things were 'bright and beautiful' especially 'the purple headed mountain and the river running by.' It was an artist's palette of colour. If the end of the world was to happen this was the place to be.

Back home I busied myself with normal tasks and then sitting by the window that gave me a view of the mountain I so loved and the fields of lush green grass where the sheep grazed I picked up my pen and began to write; my head was full of words inspired by my afternoon on the mountain. Only one thing marred my contentment and that was the thought of that meteor devastating my beautiful valley.

We were taking our usual walk but it wasn't such a beautiful day as there was a heaviness in the atmosphere; a feeling of doom and gloom, Bruno did not race on ahead but walked doggedly by my side. Why today was the going so hard? I felt that I was taking three steps forward and two steps back. Finally we reached the summit and looking down on the valley it was shrouded in a mist. Then I caught a glimpse of what I thought was the sun but it appeared to flash through the heavens lighting up the sky was this the meteor that was going to put an end to man-kind? In the distance hearing the ringing of alarm bells I began to panic; here on the top of the mountain surely this would be the first place a meteor would land. Although I felt panic stricken I realised I must hide; tightening Bruno's lead in my grasp I crouched down and crawled through the orifice between the boulders pulling Bruno with me. Once my eyes became accustomed to the dimness of the cavern I realised it went way back into the bowels of the mountain-side. Was it just old mine workings or a burial chamber of our ancient ancestors?

How long would I have to stay hidden in the depths of the earth before it would be safe to go out? My stomach ached from sitting in a cramped position or was it pangs of hunger? It seemed hours that I had sat there in the darkness but finally I made up my mind to venture out; I found it even more difficult to crawl back it was as if my legs had weights on them and I had to drag Bruno as he made no attempt to move. As I saw a glimmer of light I made one final effort to reach the opening. I blinked my eyes the light was so bright; as I got to my feet Bruno ran off; I tried to call him but my voice remained silent; was it the shock of what I beheld.

No longer was the grass green or the heather purple and the fronds of the ferns were charred black as was the whole of the valley before me. The carnage was worse than any I had seen of the devastation left after bombs had been dropped during the war. No houses remained standing and the river had disappeared. The land appeared to have been flattened; I wandered aimlessly as there was no path to follow; surely by now I should be where the village once stood but there was nothing no ruins and where were all the people as there was no sign of bodies neither human nor animal. Surely, I wasn't the only person left alive? Without food and water I too would surely suffer an agonizing death at least those that had not escaped the blast would have died instantly.

How vast an area had been devastated by the blast or was it just this valley? I must travel on and try and find help but I was so tired I really must rest but I must find Bruno.

'Bruno', I called. 'Bruno where are you?' I felt his heavy paws upon my chest and his slobbering kisses upon my face. The bright light had all but disappeared with the exception of a faint glow in the distance. Bruno's slobbering seemed to bring me to my senses; where was I? Gradually I focussed my eyes on the distant light; surely that was a street light and then realization dawned upon me I was in my bedroom and it had all been a bad dream; more than just a dream a night-mare. Had I really taken to heart what I had heard on the radio?

Later that day I told my friend about my bad dream and was really surprised when she began to laugh.

'It is nothing to laugh about it was quite scary and the thought that such an event could happen any day is really distressing.'

'If you hadn't turned the radio off you would have realized that a panel had been discussing a new book and one of them had been reading a section from it. I found it boring and didn't even take note of the title.'

'I certainly won't be reading it; my dream was scary enough.'

It really had upset me to the degree that Bruno and I avoided the mountain for quite a while.

The End

Val Baker Addicott

My Guardian Angel

As I stepped out into the cold night air the hospital doors swung closed behind me. My shift should have finished two hours previously but there had been so many admitted that evening; terrible casualties of the bombing raids that every bed was in use even overflowing into the corridors. There was a frightening silence; fires were burning in the city giving cause for alarm as it lit the way for the next air-raid that was surely to follow. This had been going on night after night since the 7th September. No-one was safe as on the 10th September St. Thomas' had been hit by a bomb and nurses killed. I pulled up the collar of my coat as the night was cold. The moon shone brightly and the stars filled the heavens. I would soon be home and I knew mother would have kept something warm for my supper. The search lights scanned the skies and then at the same time as I heard the air-raid siren I also heard a dull drone in the distance; surely not again we had suffered enough. I seemed to be the only person on the bridge and as I looked for the big 'S' for a shelter I realized they were almost above me. I was so scared I felt as if I looked up I would look straight into the eyes of our enemy as the planes were flying low. I could see their reflection in the river below I didn't know what to do so I sat down against one of the buttresses hoping it would hide me.

I began to pray; 'Dear God save me I am too young to die; there are people in hospital who need me; my mother needs me; please, please God help me.' I could hear the blasts from the bombs and the sirens of the fire-engines. Here was I praying for myself and all those people also needed help. 'Please God save us.'

I sensed that someone was standing looking down on me; 'Come young lady you can't stay there. You need help?'

Had I spoken my prayer aloud; had he heard me? I looked up expecting to see an air-raid warden but this man was not in uniform; he was young and at first glance appeared to be very handsome. The bombers were still flying over-head and I was more scared than ever. 'I want to stay here as they will see us.'

'Come you will be safe with me I promise.'

There was something comforting in his voice so I stood up but I was still trembling and so afraid.

He put his arm around my shoulders; it was an act of familiarity but it didn't bother me as suddenly I felt safe and comforted. I felt as if I was cocooned in a shroud that hid me from the enemy overhead.

We walked silently across the bridge and then down the road that led to my home. The 'all-clear' had sounded and the street was a hive of activity; fire-engines, ambulances, A.R.P. wardens what terrible destruction the last raid had left in its wake. I began to pray silently that my mother was safe. No-one stopped me as we continued down the street.

My home was in darkness as was the norm due to the black-out but the house a few doors down was in flames. 'Dear God I hope no-one is hurt.' I spoke the words aloud.

'If you truly believe God will answer your prayers. Do not lose faith Samantha God will answer your prayers.'

'Would you like to come in I am sure my mother will have the kettle boiling.'

'Thank you but I will say 'Goodnight'.

'It is I that should be thanking you.'

'Just doing my job. Until we meet again.'

I opened the door and entered the warmth of my home and the stranger, as that was what he was as he hadn't told me his name, disappeared into the mass of people who were also doing all they could to help.

I was glad to see sitting by my mother's kitchen table Mrs. Fielding and her young child was in my mother's arms.

Another of my prayers had been answered that night and when I told my mother she just smiled and said; 'Someone was watching over you perhaps it was your guardian angel.'

Before blowing out my candle I said my prayers and thanked God for the stranger who protected me and for saving Mrs. Fielding and her baby and lastly to watch over my father who was in some far away land.

Night after night the relentless bombing of our country continued. So many people were made homeless as the count of destroyed or damaged homes escalated to the one million mark. Mother decided that as she had some spare rooms she would take in lodgers. She had already rented a room to Mrs. Fielding and suggested that I spread the word around the hospital. There had been a time when I had loved nursing but at this terrible time it was so heart-breaking as one tried to help save the lives of these brave people; not just the fact that there were limbs lost; eye sight impaired; and wounds that wouldn't heal so many were mentally damaged after losing not just their homes but their families; wives, husbands, parents and children. Although the city streets seemed void of children playing after their evacuation to the country many still remained. No longer did we keep regular shifts we just worked around the clock doing all we could to keep our patients comfortable. Who would have ever thought that the basement of our hospital would be filled with patients and an operating theatre? Hospital basements filled with beds and underground stations with people seeking a night's shelter from the bombing. I hated being in the basement but I was needed; just doing my job a small cog in the big wheel.

As I lived near to the hospital I chose not to board in the nurses' quarters; walking home in day-light one could see the reality of the damage the air raids had left. Not just homes but shops, churches and on 13th September even Buckingham Palace had been hit by a bomb.

How many nights had we suffered these raids? Thirty, forty nights of torture but we as a nation were resilient we tried our best to continue a normal life; greeted each day with a smile and a helping hand for our neighbour and just hoped that the next bomb that fell from the sky didn't have our name on it.

I had been visiting a friend who had just given birth to a bouncing baby boy. I was on duty at six o'clock and as I made my way back to the hospital all appeared to be quiet; the city was alive with the hustle and bustle of traders packing up their wares; A.R.P. wardens checking that black-out blinds shut out every chink of light. Firemen still fighting to put out the last burning embers of fires from the previous night's raid. Policemen directing people to underground stations and to their homes; as all signs had been taken down. I hoped and prayed that I would get safely to the hospital and then the inevitable happened the air-raid siren let out its frightening screech. 'The tube station just around the corner is the best place', said a friendly warden but before I had gone a few yards I could see a bomb dropping from the sky; 'Oh! God dear God don't let this one have my name on it.' I heard the deafening explosion as it landed a few yards from where I stood frozen to the spot. I wanted to pray but the only words that came to me were the Lord's Prayer.

The blast from the bomb knocked me backwards and flying debris came from all directions; splinters of glass, pieces of timber landed on me but I felt no hurt. I opened my eyes and looked up to the heavens planes were still flying over-head and I could hear the sound of explosion after explosion; we were in for another bad night.

'Dear God protect my family and friends.' I must get up but I was too afraid.

'Come Samantha we must get you to hospital.'

The warden must have seen the name badge on my coat. 'I don't want to go to hospital I want to go home'. I took his outstretched hand; it was the same man who had helped me previously. 'It is you.'

'I told you I would always be there for you. Come let us make our way.'

'Shouldn't we go to a shelter?'

'Just across the bridge and you will be safely home with your mother.'

I felt as though a spell had been cast over me; the planes were flying low over-head and bombs were dropping all over the city; I was waiting for someone to fire at us but we crossed the bridge as if cloaked in a canopy of protective armour. Once again I was home safely; the stranger left me at the door and his last words were; 'Follow your heart', He turned and disappeared into the smoke of the burning fires.

Mother bathed my cuts and bruises and couldn't believe how lucky I had been. I was off work for a few days as I had a terrible headache from the bump on the back of my head but other than that it had been a miracle that nothing worse had happened to me as I was sure that bomb had my name on it.

As she poured me a second cup of tea she had said; 'Your Guardian Angel protected you again.'

'Do you really believe that mother?'

'My dear old granny always said that when we are born we are given a Guardian Angel who protects us from harm.'

'It is a lovely thought mother but what about all the people just in this country who are dying and injured every day?'

'I expect it is a busy time for our Guardian Angels.' Mother had an answer for everything.

Fifty seven days the bombing had continued relentlessly but Britain had remained strong and undeterred we would, like the Phoenix, rise from the ashes. The threat of invasion was over now we must unite as one and win the battle.

Just before Christmas mother received a letter from a doctor at the hospital where I worked; he was replying to the advert that I had posted on the notice board; mother was content with his references so had replied saying that the room was his and not to forget to bring his ration book.

'That's all my rooms filled; good thing Mrs. Fielding is helping me out.'

'When are you expecting him?'

'Friday afternoon.'

It was my late shift on Friday and when I arrived home mother said that her new lodger had retired to his room but she was sure I would like him as he was a very nice gentleman.

The next morning as I entered the dining room carrying a breakfast tray I almost dropped it in amazement as sitting by the table was the man who had come to my assistance. 'It is you.' I stammered.

He rose from his chair; 'Sorry, there must be some misunderstanding I don't believe we have met; Dr. Graham Knight.' He held out his hand.

'But...' I continued to stammer, 'on the bridge you saved me from the bombs'.

'It would have been an honour to have saved you but I only arrived in London last week. Was looking for lodgings saw your poster and here I am.'

His stature; his looks were the double of the man who saved me. Could mother possibly be right that my prayers had been answered and God had sent my Guardian Angel to protect me but who had guided Dr. Graham Knight to my home; I began to wonder was there a reason for him being here.

Mother's lodgers must have enjoyed the care and comforts she bestowed upon them as they stayed with us and were a happy band of brothers as with the exception of Mrs. Fielding they were all men. The dining room table was for serving food at meal times but every evening out would come the old games; dominoes; Ludo and even snakes and ladders and of course the pack of cards. Mother wouldn't allow money to change hands so they played for matchsticks. Mother so loved her 'boys' as she referred to them.

By the beginning of spring Graham and I were beginning to get closer to each other. During the winter months we had sat in the sitting room and as we were both avid readers we would discuss the books we had read and were reading but now it was spring and when free from our hospital duties we would take walks along the river band and into the parks. How well I remember our first kiss and then from just walking side by side we held hands. By the summer we both knew that our love was true and Graham asked me to marry him. Do I need to say that mother was delighted; 'Something told me the first time I saw him that he was the man for you; your knight in shining armour.' Excuse the pun she jested.

It was our wedding day and luckily father was on leave and as I walked down the aisle on my father's arm on a beautiful September day I felt an arm around my shoulder and knew that my Guardian Angel was also there by my side.

The End

Tea for Two

I had worked at the Manor for over ten years; rising from scullery maid to lady's maid but now I was tired of my job and so longed for change. I was fed up of being a servant and treated like something the dog brought in; bowing and curtsying; fetching and carrying and for what? Just a small pittance of a wage. I hated the grime and squalor of the small town. Everywhere one looked all that was visible to the eye were slag heaps and mine workings. Men in their work clothes covered in coal dust and women in their well-worn ragged attire. The only time they put on their best was on a Sunday or to attend someone's funeral or wedding. Mother was often cross with me and said I had ideas above my station and needed pulling down a peg or two.

I had been born and bred in the small mining town. Went to school and played on the slag heap with my friends; all in all I had had a happy childhood. Day in day out always the same routine for mother. Monday wash day; Tuesday ironing; Wednesday cleaning; Thursday she visited friends especially anyone who was sick or had just given birth, Friday shopping and Saturday baking ready for Sunday. Sunday, had for as long as I can remember, always been the same; Chapel in the morning; Sunday School in the afternoon and then the Evening Service. It was on a walk with friends after Sunday School that I had my first kiss; the pleasure of being kissed by the one village boy that all the girls worshipped was also marred as word had got back to mother and I was severely reprimanded and on that occasion was given the facts of life. How could kissing a boy get me pregnant? I suppose you could say her lecture scared me.

It was about this time that I started work at the Manor; I had just had my 15th birthday and mother said hard work would put silly ideas out of my head. It certainly did by the time my long day ended I was ready for bed.

My teenage years rolled by; I often felt depressed when I heard of all my school friends getting married and having babies. I visited my parents every Sunday and was still treated like a child and had to abide by their rules. Mother had even chosen a suitable companion to walk out with me after Chapel; her close friend's son but when he began to get to familiar with me by kissing me and trying to fondle my breasts I soon put a stop to that. Word must have gone around that I was frigid because I never got asked out again.

I have just had my 25th birthday; mother baked me a cake and gave me a locket that had belonged to my grandmother. I suppose by what I have said you will think my parents were unkind but I realise that they were strict but really did love me and only wished to protect me. I am still young but feel I will end up a spinster and someone's maiden aunt. There is no-one left in my circle of friends that I would consider as a suitable partner so all I can do is continue working at the Manor and waiting on others.

I had resigned myself to a servant's life. It didn't help my longing for change when, as a lady's maid, a few times a year I would travel with my lady either to the city or to posh country homes. We had just returned from a long week-end in London where my lady had visited the theatre and had held a large house party in her London home.

'I am rather exhausted Clara; your services won't be required for a few days so take this opportunity and spend them with your mother.'

The setting sun made the hillside around the manor look beautiful but below lay the town shrouded in a mist of chimney smoke and coal dust. The smell was quite nauseating and my spirit ebbed. Mother always put my low spirits down to 'the time of the month'; little did she know that they were always with me.

Mother appeared to be in an agitated mood. 'It been burning a hole in me since it arrived on Friday; it can only mean trouble.'

'What has upset you mother?'

'That letter on the mantle-piece; it is addressed to you just hate seeing letters in official looking brown envelopes.'

I took down the letter and taking a knife sliced it open; my eyes skimmed the contents but I had to sit down to read it carefully as what I saw stunned me, to say the least, I was in shock. If this was true my dreams had become a reality.

'It is from Aunt Maud's solicitor she died a month ago and left everything to me.'

Mother's face was ashen; 'That blasted woman even in death she still torments me. You must write back and tell them you can't take it.'

I had never seen mother in such a temper. Aunt Maud was father's elder sister and in all my years I had never met her. When I once found a photo of her mother had ripped it up and threw it on the fire. Never again was Aunt Maud's name mentioned.

This inheritance was a dream come true why should I turn it down it was a means of getting away from my depressing existence. I must stand my ground.

'Mother it would mean a better life for all of us; dad won't have to work in the mine and life for you will be so much easier.'

Mother continued to raise her voice; 'You might be ashamed of your life-style but this is father and my home since the day we got wed and here we will stay. Go to the big town and be damned you are just like her a stuck up bitch. Pack your bags and get out before father comes home; go to your posh mistress and tell her you are leaving.'

'But mother....'

'Get out,' she screamed; 'after all we have done for you. Just go get out of my sight.'

'Ten of the Best'

There was no reasoning with her so I quickly went to my room and packed my few meagre possessions. Before I left I tried kissing her but she pushed me away.

'I knew this would happen I told him the day would come.'

Perhaps I should have gone to the Manor and worked my notice but I was upset by mother's reaction; I had just had my pay and also a few pound in my purse so I went directly to the station and bought a ticket; my destination was just twenty miles away but to me it meant new beginnings. Every town and city seemed to have a 'Railway Hotel' and the one I approached looked rather splendid so as it was getting late I booked a room for the night. Luckily, my coat was one of my Lady's 'hand me downs' so although with very limited funds I looked financially affluent.

'Will madam require supper?'

I had been to many posh places with my Lady so I asked for a tray to be sent to my room.

I slept well and after taking breakfast in the vast dining room I asked for directions to the solicitor's office. I was wary of visiting the office as I hadn't made an appointment but their letter had stated to call at their office at my convenience. A very young man was sitting by a large desk; as soon as I gave my name he said 'I will inform Mr. Griffiths that you are waiting.'

What I learnt sitting in Mr. Griffiths' office really shocked me. He made me welcome; told me I was now quite a wealthy young woman; he also informed me that there were legal papers to sign but firstly, a letter to read from my Aunt. Mr. Griffiths asked his clerk to bring tea for us and then handed me the letter.

There was one neatly written sheet of paper and also a folded document. I began to read the letter then looked at Mr. Griffiths in amazement. So many things in my young life now made sense.

'Perhaps you would like something stronger Miss Walters?'

I most certainly did I couldn't believe what I had read but on opening the folded document it revealed a birth certificate; it was mine Aunt Maud was my biological mother and also on there was my father's name William John Morris and in brackets deceased. Aunt's letter had said that I had been conceived in love but they were to be married but my father, a soldier, had been killed in the second Boar War in 1900 so her brother and his new wife agreed to take the baby and raise the child as their own to avoid any disgrace on the family.

Mr. Griffiths suggested he took me to the house he also suggested that among Miss Maud's paper's I would be able to piece together more of her life.

I was surprised to find that the house; a very elegant villa was on a beautiful tree lined avenue just a short walk from the busy centre and next door to an antique shop. To say I was excited would fall short of the truth I was just bursting with delight. Everything was just perfect. The furniture was old but elegant; the drapes on the windows were luxurious every room was a delight to the eye. The dresser filled with sparkling blue and white delft china. I just couldn't believe all this was mine.

'Can I really stay here tonight?'

'Of course you can it is all yours.'

'I left my case at the Station Hotel.'

'I will send my clerk for it. We supervised the cleaning of the property in readiness for you. Miss Walters had a cleaning lady who came in a few times a week I am certain she will be pleased if you keep her on I believe it would be Miss Walters' wish.'

It took me quite a while to take everything in; I wrote to my 'parents' as that is how I would always think of them but received no reply. I kept Mrs. Roberts on as my 'daily' as I found her a delightful middle aged lady.

This was the life going to bed when I felt the need and rising sometimes at mid-day. I was happy but there was something missing. I had no friends perhaps if I found a suitable job but what was 'suitable' I had no qualifications all I could do was take care of a Lady; her clothes, her hair, bring her breakfast and afternoon tea.

I decided to cheer myself I would go for a walk to the park but just as I passed the neighbour's antique shop I noticed a sign in the window. **'ASSISTANT REQUIRED WITH SOME KNOWLEDGE OF ANTIQUES'**

I had no educated knowledge about antiques but had been surrounded by them all my years at the Manor and now my home was full of them.

Here goes I had nothing to lose. As I entered the shop the bell above the door jiggled merrily and through an open door to my left I could see another room an exact copy of my sitting room but to my amazement filled from floor to ceiling with antiques; chairs, china, glass, silver it was like Aladdin's cave.

'Good afternoon madam can I be of assistance.'

My, Oh! My. My heart missed a few beats I had never met such a handsome man. To say 'tall, dark and handsome' would not be sufficient adjectives for the man who came down the stairs. Even in those first few minutes I decided that he must be in his early forties.

'I have come about the advert in the window.'

'I had forgotten that was still there I've given up on finding someone.'

'Sorry to have bothered you I was just passing.'

He seemed flustered; 'Do come through take a seat as you see there are plenty available. My mother and I ran the business together but sad to say she has been taken ill and is now bed ridden. I have a nurse coming in to attend to her but I am sorry to say she needs a lot of attention and I cannot do both. What is your knowledge of antiques?'

Okay I was going to be honest I already liked what I saw about this man and didn't want to give him a false impression. 'Nothing.'

'Why ask about the job if you know nothing about antiques?'

'I have been surrounded by them for many a year and now my new home is filled with them; by the way, I live next door. I am Miss Walter's niece.' One small white lie wouldn't hurt.

'Maud Walters was my mother's close friend; small world.'

'I could easily learn about antiques from books.'

'The business isn't doing well it needs a new face I am sure you will be just perfect. Hours to suit us both if you agree.'

So started an amiable business relationship with Luke Pritchard and myself. I enjoyed sorting through the antiques and making everything look more attractive but business did not improve. The winter was bad and less and less people came to the shop. I had offered to help with his mother but she insisted that only the nurse and Luke attend her.

A freezing cold January morning brought Luke to my front door. Why does one always say the wrong thing? 'Come in out of the cold you'll freeze to death standing there.'

'Clara it's my mother she died in the night; I am waiting for the undertakers but the roads are so bad.'

I noticed that he was trying hard to hold back his tears. I put my arms around him; 'Don't hold back the tears from me you just cry it will help.'

'I adored her Clara but these last months have been hell is it wrong of me to say I am glad it is all over.'

'She is no longer suffering Luke.' My arms were still around him and his head was on my breast as we sat together on the sofa.

Spring came and Luke and I had formed a close bond but there was no romance; well, not on Luke's part but deep down I knew that I had fallen in love with this wonderful man.

One Saturday evening we were sitting in my parlour. We often had a meal together on a Saturday. 'I had better make a move Clara just need to get this off my chest but if business doesn't improve I will have no option but to sell up.'

'I've been thinking but haven't said anything as I didn't wish to interfere. I've walked this avenue many times and have observed the properties; there are family homes but there are also offices and where there are offices there are staff who need refreshment. My idea was to turn your adjacent room into a tea shop. You have a kitchen at the back that would need modernizing and you might have to take on someone who can cook. You can run the antique business and I the tea shop.' Had I said too much?

'It will cost money to do that and until business bucks up I haven't got it; my money is tied up in the antiques.'

'The only way business will improve is to draw people in. I have money and I am willing to go into business with you.'

'You will do that for me? Why?'

What was I to say? That I had fallen in love with him? Here goes; deep down I felt he cared about me but something was holding him back. 'Luke Pritchard is your blood made of ice and your heart made of stone? You asked me 'why? Haven't you any idea? I think I fell in love with you the moment I saw you coming down those stairs and when I held you in my arms when your mother died I knew at that moment that I really did love you.'

He just sat there and gazed at me in amazement and then he said 'You love me? How I have longed to hear those words but I was afraid that if I told you how I felt you would leave as I am too old for you. There must be twenty years between us.'

'So what difference does that make?' I put my arms around his neck and hugged him but it didn't stop there. His hungry lips were upon mine and two people who had been starved of love soon found it impossible to control their emotions.

He fumbled with the buttons on my blouse and when he began to caress my breasts it was all too much my love for him was like a bomb waiting to explode. As I led him up the stairs to my bedroom a thought flashed through my mind about how my biological parents must have felt. He continued to kiss me as he undressed me and lying naked upon the bed I watched him remove his clothes. I had never seen a man's naked body but what I saw thrilled me I knew what love-making was all about but couldn't quite understand how it would happen. He teased and tormented me and I reached such a point of excitement that when the final act took place I was amazed how easily he entered me. If this was love I wanted more.

We spent the night in each other's arms sleeping and waking and again making love and each time it delighted me even more.

The Church Bells woke us late on the Sunday morning. I still hadn't got used to having a bathroom with hot and cold running water and not just the old tin bath in front of the fire once a week. I filled the bath and then called to Luke 'Come on sleepy head do you want to share my bath.'

We took a walk in the park that afternoon and whilst feeding the swans on the lake Luke took my hand; 'Listen to the Church bells; would you like them to be rung on your wedding day? Clara will you marry me?'

We went ahead with the plans for the tea-room. Many changes were made to Luke's property. The bedrooms were turned into rooms for the antiques to be displayed for customers to view more easily. We advertised both the antiques side of the business and the tea-rooms.

With the opening of our tea rooms came our young male chef and two waitress dressed in suitable attire to represent out Edwardian style tea rooms. With the expansion of my waist-line Luke had teased that the pretty frilly apron wouldn't fit.

I had invited my adoptive parents to the wedding and had said that I would be honoured if he would walk me down the aisle; the wedding was to take place on the second Saturday in July. If they didn't attend the only guests we would have would be my cleaning lady; the two young waitresses and the chef. I hoped my solicitor and his wife would accept my invite and Luke had invited a few of his closest relatives.

I didn't feel that it was proper to wear white as my rounded belly was proof that I was no virgin. The 1920's fashions suited me well I chose an ivory full length skirt with a lace overlay and luckily with an elasticated waist and the matching smock like top concealed the fact that I was three months pregnant. A picture hat the shade of milky coffee and stylish shoes finished my ensemble. Luke had said that he would be certain to choose the right flowers for me. As for our wedding breakfast Luke and our chef had made plans to close the tea-rooms and put on a spread fit for royalty.

My poor darling Luke spent the night before our wedding on a made up bed on an antique sofa in the shop. I hadn't had a reply from my mother so was surprised that they turned up on the Friday afternoon. Little was said but by her emotions I could tell that all was forgiven on both our parts. She had even brought a gift from my Lady at the Manor so she had also forgiven me for leaving her in the lurch.

I had not told my mother about the baby so was surprised when preparing for my wedding mother came and offered to pin my hair up for me. 'You always had beautiful hair I so loved putting it in ringlets. You were such a beautiful baby when is your baby due?'

'Christmas time; I didn't know how to tell you I thought you wouldn't approve.'

'I couldn't have children that is why we took you when Maud lost William it would have been a big family scandal. You know we loved you dearly Clara. I suppose we fell out with Maud because of her life-style. Without a baby to care for and with the money that William had left her she became a successful fashion designer. Anyhow, it is all water under the bridge. We both just wish you every happiness.'

We hugged each other and I noticed that mother had tears in her eyes. 'I am not a snob mother I just wanted a better life for myself as I thought that I would never find anyone who would marry me. Now I have found the most loving, caring man in the whole world and we are so happy.'

Luke had arranged for a chauffeur driven car to take me to the Church and just before I was ready to leave the florist delivered a beautiful bouquet of cream tea roses; as promised his choice was perfect also a buttonhole of a cream rose bud and fern for dad and a spray of cream rosebuds for mother.

Just as he had promised the Church bells rang out as I stepped from the car. Mother went on ahead as father took my arm; 'You look beautiful; happy the bride that the sun shines on.' The sun was certainly shining it was a glorious day. As we walked down the path to the Church there were a few well-wishers standing on the grass verge.

I knew our love was true but I was still nervous when I walked back down this path I would be another person I would be Luke's wife; Mrs. Pritchard. I prayed silently that I would be a loving wife and mother.

The organ music filled my ears and I clung tightly to father's arm I felt weak at the knees and I was trembling from head to toe but every step I took was one closer to my beloved. He was so handsome; his smile filled my heart with love.

Our vows exchanged, the register signed and together we walked out into the sunshine to a peal of Church bells and a shower of confetti.

When our guests had left we sat together in our tea-room and opening a bottle of champagne we toasted each other and then toasted our new business that was beginning to show a profit. 'To our tea-room,' said Luke, 'to 'Tea for Two'.'

'That is a great name for it as it is two businesses in one. Soon my darling it will be tea for three or maybe four who knows. My bed is calling darling time we went home. Hope you haven't forgotten this is our wedding night.'

'How could I possibly forget that my beautiful bride I want to make mad passionate love to you all night.' As we made our way to bed Luke began to sing; *'Just tea for two; and two for tea; just me for you and you for me alone.'* The song that was on everyone's lips.

The End

Val Baker Addicott

The House on the Hill

The End

"Well that's the end of her; she has been a worry to Dora ever since she went to that house; come on Joe let's go and have a pint with the others before we head home."
"Not a very good 'turn-out' for her; by the way what are you going to do with the house? It should fetch quite a bit or will you rent it; but I suppose it will be better to sell it to a stranger as no local would want to live in that 'God-forsaken hole'. Is it true what everyone is saying that she drowned?"
"Yes, it has been assumed that she was going to market in the horse and trap and the bridge collapsed and she got thrown out into the deluge of the flood waters; the funny thing is the horse managed to get to the other side. A bit mysterious if you ask me. As for the house I don't know what is going to happen as we were surprised

that her solicitor is coming at four to read the will; I hope the stupid bitch hasn't done anything daft."

Hiding in the bushes that surrounded the grave-side she started to laugh; 'stupid bitch am I; just you wait Peter Walker and you will find out how clever I really am.'

"Where the hell did that wind come from?" said Peter turning up his jacket collar.

"What wind? I didn't feel anything there isn't even a breeze; they say it is the hottest July we've had for years."

'I'll show them', she thought and passing close to the two men she gave out a raucous laugh.

'You are right Pete I felt it then;' he too turned up the collar of his jacket as she continued to laugh.

"My God Joe she has come back to haunt us; there isn't a quiver of the leaves on the trees yonder. Let's get the hell out of here."

"Now you are being an idiot; she dead and buried and there are no such thing as ghosts. It is just a fluke wind."

Once more she circled around them and following them down the path that led from the grave-side she darted in between them and blew in their faces a cold breath; 'see you later my dear brother-in-law; you are in for a big shock; might give you a heart-attack and then you will be joining me.'

"My, it has turned cold; I feel a sudden chill. Let's go and have a few pints."

"Perhaps we are in for a storm but what amazes me there isn't a cloud in the sky."

Once again emitting a cold breath over them she circled around and saying; 'I'll be waiting for you Peter Walker I just can't wait to see your face when my will is read;' she left them and transported herself to her sister's home.

"I hate grave-yards; the very thought of all those dead bodies lying in their crypts really scares me; wouldn't want to be here at night-fall when they say the dead walk."

"Shut up; you silly old fool, they are dead as door-nails you've been reading too many of those 'Penny Dreadful' stories."

Back at her sister's home she placed herself on the fender of the newly black-leaded grate; 'my house-proud sister' she thought; for as long as she could recall her sister would only light a fire in the parlour at Christmas time. 'Hope she won't light one today or I will be in a very hot place but there I am sure that is where she will be wishing me by the end of the afternoon.' She laughed at her own humorous thought.

"Has some-one left the back door open I just felt such a draft?" Said old granny Walker as she contentedly rocked away in Peter's favourite chair.

"Don't be silly mother-in-law it is absolutely boiling in here."

"I'd like a drink; a nice bottle of stout and hurry up with it girl."

"We're waiting for the men; you know they have to be served first."

"My Peter wouldn't deprive his mother of a bottle of stout; hurry along girl or I will die of thirst and it is so hot in here there's not a breath of air think we're in for a storm."

"No pleasing the silly old bat she just said there was a draft and now she is complaining she's hot; once we get

Sylvia's money Peter and I are off; we're going to get a nice little cottage by the sea-side." Dora said to her neighbour. "See how she'll cope without us."

'The old bat has hit the nail on the head', thought Sylvia as she perched herself on the back of the rocking chair; 'there certainly is a storm brewing'. In a jovial mood she began to make the rocking chair move faster on its rockers; how she would have liked to have tipped the old woman, whom she had always detested, onto the hearth. Instead she blew cold air down the back of her neck.

"Someone has left that door open again; there is a hell of a draft here."

"It is only me mother and the lads; we stopped off for a pint and on the way up the hill we met the solicitor." Said Peter as he entered the room

"Did you bring me a bottle of stout; I asked Dora ages ago and she said I couldn't have one."

"You can drink stout all day long, mother dear, after the will is read. We should have a nice packet from the sale of that house. Come on lads let's get to the table and tuck in all of you. Let's drink a toast to the bitch who is going to make us rich." He raised his glass and just as he said. "To the bitch", she bumped his arm and the ale tipped down his best suit and over the white table cloth. He turned to his wife, who was pouring Joe a cup of tea; "watch what you doing you clumsy woman good thing it wasn't boiling tea."

"I was nowhere near you; it is you who are the clumsy one been drinking too much again. I'll be glad to get you away from your old cronies."

How Sylvia longed to tip up the tea-pot down Dora's best dress but that might cause a serious accident so instead she turned her attention back to Peter who was trying to mop up the tipped ale. 'Want another bottle?' she breathed over him but this time her breath was hot and it made Peter's face redden and in the next instant she brushed against the bottle of ale he had just opened and up-tipped it into his lap.

"You clumsy oaf," shouted his wife; "I just had your suit cleaned and look at the mess you've made."

Joe burst out laughing; "Pete can't hold his liquor he has just wet himself."

He tried to get up but Sylvia now sat on his shoulder and with every attempt she pushed him back.

He turned to his friend Joe; "She is here Joe I can feel her presence; I didn't tip that bottle."

"You need to see a shrink old pal; we just buried her so how can she possibly be here?"

"I didn't mean *her;*" he stressed the word; "I mean her spirit; I can feel her all around me."

'Dare she', thought Sylvia but she didn't think about it for long and with an extra effort she pulled the chair from under Joe and as she roared with laughter her breath exhaled across the two men and Dora; sending a chill that made them shiver.

"Told you," said Peter; "I told you she was here."

As the old grand-father clock struck the hour of four the solicitor rose from his chair and tapping on his empty glass with a fork he said; "I am here on the request of Miss Sylvia Roberts to read her last will and testament." He sat back down and moving the plates and cutlery he picked up his brief case, that he had placed on the floor by the side of his chair; opening it he took out a single sheet of paper.

"Not much on that paper Dora, my love, our fortune awaits us."

The solicitor lowered his glasses on his nose and glared at Peter with his bird-like eyes; "May I continue? It will not take me long and I will be away. The will is very simple."

"Just like her," muttered Dora and quickly put her hand to her face as she felt a sharp pain in her ear.

'Simple am I just you wait Dora Walker.'

"As I was saying."

"Well spit it out man we're wasting good drinking time."

"Miss Roberts has left all her estate in the hands of her solicitors Dobson, Dobson and McIntire to be used at their discretion in the upkeep of Hill House for it to be maintained as it was on her demise. There is a clause that she has requested must not be read but acted upon when the time arises. I will now bid you 'Good day'." Closing his briefcase and picking up his hat off the coat hook he made his departure.

'Now for the thunder-storm', thought Sylvia. It wasn't long in coming; soon the air was blue and how she laughed when they wished her to suffer long and join the devil in Hades. She swirled around the room like a puff of smoke and tipping up a plate of sandwiches a few more bottles of beer and dropping a cream cake on old granny Walker's best silk dress she made her departure and returned to the house on the hill and to her beloved where they would at last be united. She hadn't planned her death but like everything that had happened over the last decade her destiny had been planned. It was fated that they would be together and now as two spirits their happiness was complete and they would never be disturbed in the house they loved so much and she had made sure that when the time was right they would open their doors to another such lost soul as she had been.

THE BEGINNING

"Isn't it about time you got yourself a man? Peter and I would like some privacy and not have you listening in to all our conversation and everything else; I have just about had enough; we've also got to put up with the old woman."

"I have as much right to be here as you; mother left the house to both of us."

"That was before I got married. As newly-weds we need time to ourselves; we'll never have kids with you listening in it really puts Pete off. If you can't get yourself a man for goodness sake get a job; it was okay when you were caring for old Mrs. Tucker."

"Well, we knew she wouldn't live for-ever; she was nearly ninety when I went to care for her. So tell me, *dear sister*" she made a point of emphasizing the words; "where did you expect me to live after her death?"

"Go and make yourself useful; it is Monday and I have a pile of washing to do as that old hag has wet her bed again."

Sylvia picked up the laundry basket and leaving her sister still complaining went to peg out the clothes. As she hung the clothes on the garden line she mulled over her sister's words. She really did hate living here; between old granny Walker constantly complaining and unable to sleep at night listening to the moaning and groaning coming from the next room and the rattling of the old bedstead. What they were up to every night left very little to the imagination.

The washing hung out to dry; her bedroom tidied and not feeling up to any more arguments with her sister she decided to take herself off to the next town to see if she could find a job as she was now beginning to feel that if she didn't her sister would take action and kick her out and that would surely mean the workhouse for her.

"I'm off out; anything you need?"

"Yes, you out of this house; if you know what is good for you don't bother to come back."

To save on the bus fare she decided to take the mountain road to the next town; some five miles distant, as the crow flies. The route was familiar to her so she couldn't understand, on seeing a house she had never previously noticed, how she could have taken the wrong path that had taken her up a rather steep hill. Feeling quite exhausted she sat on a bolder and took in the panoramic view of the surrounding country-side. Surely, from this vantage point she would be able to see the next town but all she could see was field after field of grazing sheep and cows and a few distant farmhouses and the river winding its way to the sea.

"Good-morning young lady; I thought you might be thirsty so I brought you a beaker of ice cold spring water from the well."

Sylvia had been deep in thought and was startled on hearing a voice. She turned and saw standing behind her an elderly lady whose mode of dress was different, to say the least. It was as if she hadn't moved into the twentieth century as her dress was early Victorian. Sylvia took the beaker of water and thanked the lady.

"Do you live in the house on the hill?" she questioned.

"Yes I have always lived there."

"How do you manage to do your shopping living so far from the town?" Sylvia felt that the lady appeared too fragile to travel far."

"I manage well; I have friends and we need very little."

Later, recalling that moment, Sylvia didn't know what had made her ask; "do you need someone to live-in and care for you?"

"Why do you ask, my dear?"

"My sister wants me to move out and if I don't find a job it will mean the work-house for me."

"Destiny has sent you here and I am sure I can speak for the others but we would love you to come and live with us. Return to us on Midsummer's Day and we will welcome you."

"How will I find this place again?"

"The spirits will guide you."

Refreshed from the pure, clear water and her rest upon the boulder Sylvia thanked the lady and promised to return on the 21st June. That would give her just a few days to make the necessary arrangements for her move.

Happily, she began to make her way down the hill and turning to wave to the lady she noticed that she had been joined by a few other people all wearing different attire as if they were a troop of travelling actors.

On her arrival home there was no welcome awaiting; her sister appeared to be in an even worse mood and old granny Walker was the worse for drink and swearing and shouting at her daughter-in-law. 'The sooner I get away from here the better', thought Sylvia as she made her way up the stairs to her room.

"Where do you think you are going? Been out skiving all afternoon; there's dinner to get before Peter gets home so get your 'glad-rags' off and get and do the spuds you lazy bitch. Don't know who is writing to you but there is a letter waiting for you on the hall table."

Sylvia retraced her steps and picking up the envelope returned to the parlour to open it.

"Lady Muck has time to sit in the parlour while muggings does all the work." Complained her sister.

Sylvia opened the envelope and read the enclosed letter a second time before getting up and making her way to her room. She took an old Gladstone bag from on top of the cupboard and then packed in it her meagre wardrobe of clothes and a few treasured possessions; a silver framed photo of her parents with her as a baby and Dora about four year old and her baby bracelet and a locket her mother had given her on her 21st birthday.

She hesitated for just a moment taking one last look around the room; they had been such a happy family what had happened to change everything?

Most likely it all started with their father's death in the coal-mine; followed shortly after by his wife whom everyone said 'had died from a broken heart'.

She called out to Dora that she was leaving but having no response she left the house without a backward glance. She had no intention of walking to the nearest town so using her last few coins she took the bus that would take her away from all the trials and tribulations that she felt living with her sister. 'She can keep the house I am going to make a new life for myself.'

She made her way to the office of Dobson, Dobson and McIntire and soon all was revealed to her. Mrs. Tucker, the old lady she had taken care of for almost ten years had no living relatives and had left everything to Sylvia.

"Well young lady I assume that you understand you are quite a wealthy young woman."

'Young lady,' she thought 'that is a compliment in itself considering I am nearer forty than thirty.'

"I'd like you to continue looking after my inheritance; I will visit you once a month but at the moment I have very little need for money as I have promised to care for an old lady who lives in Hill House."

Mr. Dobson senior stared at her with what appeared to be a look of amazement. "Did you say Hill House?

Have you the right address as I understand the house has been empty for almost twenty years? Gertrude Mitchell was our client and when she died her will stated that her estate be handled by us and used in the upkeep of Hill House but under no circumstances must it be sold. The mystery deepens because only yesterday a stranger entered our office and asked for us to arrange the re-stocking of the small-holding at Hill House with the necessary animals. Chickens, ducks a horse and trap, a few sheep, goats and a cow and the necessary implements that would be required to maintain the land. We thought he had made a mistake when he said that Miss Mitchell had sent him. My brother and I stood by the window to see which direction he took but we missed seeing him leave the office. According to Miss Mitchell's will we must carry out all instructions we receive."

She booked into a hotel and relaxed in the luxury; even if it was only for one night. She didn't sleep well as Mr. Dobson's words kept going over and over in her mind. She tried to reason out the happenings of the last few days. It did seem to be very strange; what had led her to Hill House? Where had the lady come from? The terrain had been rocky but she hadn't heard her approaching and when she had looked back she had seen about six people standing waving to her; they too seemed to have appeared from no-where. All would be solved on the morrow when she returned to Hill House.

It was a glorious Midsummer's Day; she took the bus to the nearest stop to the lane that led to the mountain and she hoped that she would find her way again to Hill House. As she alighted from the bus she noticed a fragile old man standing close by holding the reins of a horse behind which was a trap.

"Miss Robert's I have been instructed to hand over the reins to you; the horse knows his way to Hill House."

"Can I drop you off anywhere?" She offered as she thought the old man looked about to collapse.

"I have no need of a ride."

She put her bag in the trap and then climbed up and taking the reins the horse needed no encouragement as he trotted off along the lane. As she turned the corner she glanced back but there was no sign of the old man. She recalled Mr. Dobson's words' 'the mystery deepens'. She felt no trepidation as any way of life would be better than the existence she had living with her sister.

Ahead of her was the mountain path, that she had walked so many times, to the next town but it was here that the horse veered to the right and began the uphill climb through a leafy glade; the hot summer sun flickered through the branches it all felt so mystical and magical. She didn't feel alone she felt as though she was being guided to her new home. Hadn't the old lady said that the spirits would guide her home? At the end of the incline the trees thinned out and she found herself on the open mountain-side and there on the top of the hill stood her new home.

The front door was open and as she entered the hall-way she was expecting to be greeted by the old lady or one of her friends but there appeared to be no-one about. She called out; "Is there anyone at home?" but received no reply. She left her bag in the hallway and ventured further down the passage; opening a door she entered an immaculate kitchen; although in many ways it was dated but to her eyes it was just perfect. Looking through the window she could see out into the yard where chickens pecked away quite contentedly and a cat lazed in the summer sun. Hearing a dog barking made her realize that she hadn't unharnessed the horse so she quickly retraced her steps. To her amazement the horse was grazing in a field opposite and the trap had been put in the barn. 'Why hadn't anyone answered her?'

Weren't they ready to meet her or perhaps they were observing her and summing her up but where was the dear, fragile lady whom she was to care for?

She returned into the house and opened the door into the sitting room; she was mesmerized by its Victorian splendour. The drapes, the furniture, the china in the cabinets and the cosy settee that stood in the bay window. She then entered the room opposite and found it to be a dining room but here she noticed a vast difference everything in the room appeared to take her back to another era to Georgian days. She just couldn't believe her eyes. Feeling in need of respite she returned to the kitchen and was amazed to find the larder well stocked.

Previously she hadn't noticed a fire burning in the stove. She quickly filled the kettle and soon it was boiling; she left the tea brewing in the pot and returning to the larder lifted the lid of the bread bin and found a loaf of what appeared to be freshly baked bread and on the shelf under a cloche was a freshly made fruit cake. This was all too perfect. Sitting herself down she began to relax and as she poured the second cup of tea she noticed her lady in the garden. She opened the back door and crossed the yard to where the lady stood petting the cat.

"Hello my dear; I am so glad you have arrived. We want you to make yourself at home and to be happy and please do not be afraid of the spirits they come and go they will never harm you."

"What shall I call you?"

She laughed; a shrill piercing laugh; "When I was young and beautiful everyone called me Gertie; you to may call be Gertie and then I will remain young. I think you might be happy in the bedroom off the sitting room I always found it such a pleasant room and you can leave the bedrooms above for our visitors. Go finish your tea we will talk again soon."

Back in the kitchen Sylvia felt even more bemused; hadn't Mr. Dobson said that Miss Gertrude Mitchell had died some twenty years ago. There was an aura through-out the house but she wasn't afraid. It was a beautiful place and she would make it her home and if the visitors were ghosts so be it.

She returned to the sitting room and for the first time noticed the door leading to the room that Miss Gertrude said could be hers. It was delightful; far more up to-date than the other rooms; she could smell the perfume of fresh cut roses and the lace curtains blew gently in the breeze that came through the open French doors; and the late afternoon sun shone on the crystal wind catchers that hung on a rail above the doors. The French doors led out to a beautiful rose garden. Walking along the path and stopping to watch the bees sipping the nectar and covering their bodies with pollen; the butterflies on the purple buddleia and the blackbird singing so sweetly she felt, that for the first time in many a year, she was a peace with the world.

She kept the home ready for 'visitors'; the bedrooms were kept fresh and the furniture polished and everything spick and span. Occasionally she heard noises in the rooms above but she never encroached on their privacy. She often saw Miss Gertrude walking in the rose garden; and the man that had met her with the horse and trap appeared to be a daily visitor. On a few occasions the lady and gentleman that occasionally occupied the room above hers would venture into the kitchen but it took them almost a year before they spoke to her. They spoke about their time together when they were on the stage. Different 'visitors' came some stopped longer than others; they all appeared to be ancient both in their mode of dress and in age; she often wondered why there were no young 'visitors'.

She stopped by the office of Dobson, Dobson and McIntire once a month and bought a few necessities. Never once did she meet anyone she knew until a spring day about two years later she turned the corner into the High Street and literally bumped into Dora and Peter. Peter was carrying a young child and she immediately noticed Dora's swollen belly.

"Out of our way," Peter pushed her to one side; "A fine sister you turned out to be leaving us in the lurch and not so much as a 'thank you' for all Dora did for you. In the money now are you? Is your house to posh to invite us for a visit?"

"It is not my house; I run a guest house for visitors and take care of the lady who owns it."

"Liar," shouted Peter, "I hear you bought a grand house in the next valley. I understand it is open house to all the men in the neighbourhood."

She had heard enough and began to walk away from them; "Mean bitch," Peter shouted after her "didn't even give the boy a 'tanner'."

She turned to face her aggressor and opening her purse took a few notes, that she had just received from old Mr. Dobson, and handed them to Dora. "Buy something for the lad and for the baby when it arrives and please don't give any to your old man I think he has enough liquor in his belly to last a life time." She did not wait for any further comment but walked away from them and did not look back.

The following summer; on Midsummer's Day she was sitting on the garden bench outside her back door when she suddenly felt a presence and turning she expected to see one of her usual 'visitors' but instead she saw walking towards her a young man in uniform, As he drew closer she could not take her eyes off the most handsome man she had ever seen. He was not like all her other visitors who were old and grey and wore ancient dress. This man was, as the romantic novels would state, 'tall, dark and handsome'. She knew that he was a 'visitor' as he had appeared, as if out of the blue. He came towards her and the smile on his face lit up his very countenance.

"May I?" he asked as he pointed to the seat beside her.

"Certainly," she said totally enraptured by his very being.

"Miss Gertrude said that you would welcome me with open arms."

"Just like Miss Gertrude to say that. Have you travelled far?"

"From France where the battle rages and men are dying like flies. Please do not talk about it; my soul has been in torment and I have come here to find a haven with you."

How could she call the presence of Alfred Cooper in her home the love of her life? In the first few months he came and then disappeared for days on end but the closer they became the longer he stayed in his human form not as an apparition that floated in space and time.

"How can I love you," she asked as they sat together in the arbour; "and how can you say you love me? I so hate it when you leave me. Why can't you stay?"

"I do love you but I am a spirit and the only way we can be together for eternity is if you too was one of us and joined us in the spirit world. Since meeting you my soul is no longer in torment; but how I long to journey through time and space with you or stay content in Hill House and open our doors to our friends."

Many weeks passed before she saw him again and the longer they were apart the more she turned his words over and over in her mind. She had nothing to lose; the house on the hill would still be hers to come and go as she wished but she would never, ever be alone again. What had he told her? He had said that if she too was a spirit he could hold her in his arms something that he was unable to do her being human and him a ghost. The more she thought about it the more determined she became to resolve the situation.

It took great courage on her part to put into motion her plan. His visitations were becoming less frequent and she was becoming more and more lonesome without him. In the beginning they spent days and sometimes weeks together but now it was just fleeting moments. She also missed seeing Miss Gertrude and her other 'visitors'. Alfred had told her that if she was one of them they would all be a family together.

It was almost Midsummer and a storm had raged for days and she was due to go to town to visit old Mr. Dobson. She put on her water-proof cape and hitching up the horse to the trap she set off. She decided against continuing her journey when she heard the rumble of thunder; she stopped at the village and posted a letter to Mr. Dobson and then headed back for home. Suddenly, she felt his presence beside her, "I love you" she heard him whisper. "I will never leave you ever again. Miss Gertrude and the family are waiting for you."

She was crossing the bridge over the river when a sudden flash of lighting scared the horse she felt herself falling and crashing through the wooden structure of the old bridge; then she saw him and felt his arms about her as he broke her fall and then dropped her gently into the pool beneath the waterfall. "I'll be waiting for you my love; come back to us very soon."

She hated being shut in the coffin; she heard the minister's words; "Ashes to ashes; dust to dust…." She felt the weight of the soil as it was thrown on the coffin and then she was free; she left her broken body and soared up to the heavens. Returning to the shrubs that grew near to her grave she heard Peter's words; "well, that's the end of her."

As far as she was concerned it was just the beginning.

1940

The years had been happy for Sylvia and Albert; when they manifested their-selves they spent the time in Hill House and opened their doors to more and more 'visitors' but as apparitions they journeyed the land together watching over the dying and helping them along their journey to peace. On one such journey they saw a poor young woman with two small children sitting in the garden of her bombed out home. They heard her cries for 'help' and taking pity on her they resolved to do something about her terrible situation.

Sylvia took on her human form and visited the solicitors' office of Dobson, Dobson and McIntire. Mr. McIntire junior was too young to know anything about her so she just walked into his office and asked to see him urgently. She mentioned the Last Will and Testament of the late Miss Sylvia Roberts and handed him a letter saying that the time had now come to carry out Miss Roberts' last wish.

She also left with him the address of the young mother. Her job was done she had given Hill House to someone who needed it more than her and her ghostly 'visitors'. The end of the haunting of Hill House was over and no longer would Sylvia and Albert take on their human form but occasionally they would pass by just to check that the family were safe and on one happy day in 1946 they left the house on the hill forever as they saw their young woman and her children enfolded in the arms of her soldier husband.

The End

Note: First published in 2014 in
'Mammy Val's Little Book of Allsorts'

Val Baker Addicott

This Little Piggy Didn't go to Market

It was a beautiful August day; she had been elbow deep in the wash tub since early morning and had her Monday wash out on the line before her neighbours.

'Co-ee' called her neighbour as she tapped on the back door; 'Have you got the kettle on? You had your washing out before my water was hot. Did anyone wet the bed?'

Edna was well used to her friend Mildred's remarks so ignored her comment. 'I suppose you want a piece of my cherry cake with the cup of tea.'

'Are you busy this afternoon? Grand-father mentioned that we need to pick the peas and beans and the fruit also needs picking; just wondered if you cared to help? Payment in kind.'

'I would like to preserve some fruit for Christmas but as for making jam don't know if I will have enough sugar; rations don't go very far. Dig for Victory your father and grand-father certainly do that.'

'Come down to the allotment about two I'll be waiting for you.'

Edna took in her washing; damped it down and folded it ready for ironing. She went back out to her front garden and picked the last of the garden peas and dug up the last of the early potatoes; she had tried her best but was no gardener and it was hard for a woman on her own; she would prefer to see a garden full of flowers but every-one was doing their bit for the war effort. With the men away the women had to turn their hand to many a task that had always been done by the man of the house.

Tying up her hair in a head-scarf and putting on her old wellington boots she picked up the wooden trug and made her way to the allotment. The woodland garden was surrounded by a high wall and a high wooden panelled gate that was always kept locked. Edna called to her friend as she lifted the latch on the gate; 'It's only me.' She knew the garden well as the two friends had spent many a happy child-hood day sneaking into the garden and eating the fruit from the bushes and then been chased off by Mildred's grand-father. Those long hot summer days would never be forgotten but now they were young brides. Their husbands having to go to war made these two friends, with no real responsibilities, revert back to the days of their youth. They had both joined the W.I. and were busy fund raising and doing what came naturally making jams and preserves and of course the favourite cakes for fetes.

'Think I'll join the Land Army,' said Mildred as the two set about filling their baskets with the fresh produce. 'I've been brought up on the land looking after chickens and pigs since I was knee high to a grasshopper.'

'George has leave in a few weeks; I worry so as I am sure he will be sent abroad. We are hoping to start a family but if that doesn't happen I will join you.'

'If nothing happens,' laughed Mildred; 'you'll have great fun trying though. Is he good in bed? I've deduced from Tom's letters, reading between the lines, that he is up North somewhere. We didn't even get to have a wedding night.'

'Are you trying to tell me you haven't done 'it'?'

'Oh! Edna you are a one; are you that naïve? We were at 'it' as you politely stated from the moment we first met; up in the ferns and the long grass. Mother Earth was our love bed.'

'Weren't you afraid of getting pregnant?'

'Think I'll have to give you some advice on that subject; come on we need to finish this row as father wants to plant some late crops.'

'What is that noise? It sounds like a pig.'

'Hush; grand-dad doesn't want anyone to know.'

'Whose going to hear me there is only you and I here?'

'Come with me I'll show you but don't tell anyone.'

The two walked down the path almost to where the allotment joined the woodland. 'Father made a makeshift sty for Bertha from these old roofing sheets and old pit props. Do you want to see her?'

'Thought your pigs are all at the top of your back garden; why is she down here?' Edna could see a really large sow wallowing in the muddy surround. She really felt sorry for her all on her own.

'Bertha is the syndicate pig. She is having special treatment and being fattened up so that we will get a good price when we slaughter her. We have the village 'pig club' but the Government takes half when we slaughter so grandad came up with the idea of having one 'special' pig that we could make money from the 'big-wigs'.'

'Surely, if he gets caught he will be charged.'

Mildred laughed; 'the Chief Constable is one of the syndicate. Come on let's get back to work I've said too much.'

The thought of Bertha, the pig, spending her days on her own and to what end – just to be slaughtered kept Edna awake but by the morning she had come up with a plan that she hoped Mildred, who was always ready for a prank, would agree upon.

The next afternoon Edna donned her hat and coat and decided to visit her brother and family. Harry, some ten years older than Edna, was a hill farmer and from a very young age Edna had enjoyed visiting him especially at lambing time. It was quite a long walk but the day was so beautiful that it was a joy to meander along the little white road that led to the lane and then crossing the brook along the stepping stones to the sheep track to the farm. One could not ask for a view more splendid as one could see for miles from one mountain top to another and then below the valley and the river. Little houses dotted here and there that made one feel like *Gulliver* looking down upon *Lilliput*. She enjoyed the time spent with her sister-in-law and nursing the new baby made her feel quite 'broody'. She thought that if she needed any advice about making babies she would ask her sister-in-law not Mildred.

Her brother had been to market in a distant town and it was quite late before he returned. She went to meet him hoping for a ride on the old tractor as it chugged its way up the windy road. She had only travelled along this road on a few occasions; once was when Harry married Sue.

She didn't quite expect the reaction that she got when she told him of her plan. He roared with laughter; 'okay kid sister I'll go along with you if possible I will meet you by the brook.

Another restless night thinking of how she was going to persuade Mildred.

She crossed her front garden and leaning over the fence knocked on Mildred's door. 'Kettle on and I have one of Sue's fruit cakes.'

Mildred didn't need to be asked a second time.

Edna waited until her friend was eating her second piece of cake before she put her plan to her.

'Have you got anything planned for Friday night?'

'Have to check my diary; can't make up my mind if I spend the evening with *Robert Taylor; Clark Gable or Roy Rogers and Trigger.*'

'Be serious Mildred I have a plan.'

'What have you been plotting?'

'Just listen please; I was upset about poor Bertha and the condition of her sty and then I began to think about how we feel with our husbands away so I decided I wanted to save Bertha and find her a husband so that she could have lot and lots of babies.'

'I always thought you were a bit mad but this time you have really 'lost it' worrying about the sex life of a pig.'

'I told you to 'shut up' and listen. I had a word with my brother, who although he only kept sheep and a few cows, also has a young boar that he bid wrongly for at an auction. The boar is ready for a mate and if she has piglets you will be half owner; not your grand-dad or father. Your own nest egg Mildred.'

The mention of money made Mildred prick up her ears; 'Pig's egg you mean; okay I am following you but it is a mad idea how are we going to get one fat pig to your brother's farm? We'll surely get caught.'

'We know these woodland paths like the back of our hand and you always used to say you would find your way out blindfolded.'

'You must be kidding; I thought we would take her up the road.'

'Now you are being the idiot; we would surely be caught and if Bertha left a few droppings along the way what would you do about that? We'll take her out of the woodland gate and then follow the path up to the brook hopefully my brother will meet us there.'

'We will have to take a torch or how will we know where we are going?'

'No torches or we will end up having a bomb dropped on us. We will just rely on the moon and your brilliant knowledge of the footpaths; remember clever clogs you said that you could find your way out blindfolded.'

'How are we going to persuade her to come with us?'

'A bag of apples and a dog collar.'

'A dog collar you really are mad we haven't got one big enough for Bertha's neck.'

'Thought about that we can join two or three together.'

'Grand-dad's belt; with his beer pot that would certainly fit Bertha and I'll get some rope from the shed he won't miss it. Perhaps we should wear camouflage and paint our faces.'

'You watch too many movies.'

So the plan was set for the 'kidnapping' of Bertha Pig. Only one thing had been forgotten was that Mildred's father kept the big gate locked and no way could these two young ladies climb over the high garden wall; so they had to traipse down through the village praying that they wouldn't bump into the village policeman. 'If we do we'll tell him we are going to an 'all night party' to raise money for charity.'

The moon shone brightly as they wended their way through the long grass in the field behind the houses. 'I just trod in something horrible;' complained Mildred.

'Cow pat I expect; hope we don't meet a bull as I have my red jumper on.'

Suddenly the moon went behind a cloud and the two rescuers stumbled along through the muddy terrain. 'Told you we should have brought a torch. Think we are here I can just make out the back gate. Clever idea of mine to leave it unlocked. I can just here my dad and grand-dad blaming each other for not checking the gate when they find Bertha gone.'

More squelching about in mud and Bertha's waste as Edna enticed her with an apple whilst Mildred put the belt around her neck and tied on two pieces of rope so that each of them could control her.

Good thing Bertha was a greedy sow and didn't take much enticement to get her through the gate and by the time they left the field and entered the wood the moon had risen high in the heavens.

'What a stink,' said Edna 'what she is putting in one end is coming out the other all over my wellingtons.'

'Stop complaining; it was your mad idea.'

With a lot of tugging and pulling and apple feeding they had almost come to the edge of the woodland where the path would take them to the brook and hopefully where her brother would be waiting when Bertha decided that she was tired and would take a rest.

She just flopped down on the path her belly flab spreading out like an unset jelly.

'I can't move;' complained Mildred; 'she is on my foot.'

Edna tugging on the rope was to no avail Bertha wouldn't budge. She pushed on Bertha's flabby belly and Mildred removed her foot. She could not be enticed by an apple. 'Think I put some carrots in the bag if they work for a donkey they might work for Bertha.' Edna took the carrot and walked a few paces in front and then held out the carrot. 'Give her a push Mildred.'

Finally Bertha was persuaded and with a final push from the rear by Mildred she got to her feet. 'I'll need to fill the bath tub with disinfectant when I get home what a smelly pig and that is 'if' we ever get home. I can just see us getting caught and being locked up in jail.'

'Your father wouldn't do that to you.'

'He most certainly would just to teach me a lesson.'

Finally they reached the meeting point by the stepping stones but Edna's brother wasn't waiting.

'Surely we don't have to get Bertha across the stepping stones; thought there was a little bridge.'

'It got washed away with the floods last winter and hasn't been replaced as only hikers and idiots like us use it.'

It appeared that Bertha was quite happy to wade through the water as Edna crossed first followed by Bertha and Mildred at the rear. When Edna reached the opposite side she pulled on the rope to encourage

Bertha but to her horror instead of coming forward Bertha stepped backwards. Edna couldn't help but laugh as her friend slipped and ended up sitting in the water.

'Get that darned pig out before she sits on me.' At last reaching the bank Mildred emptied the water out of her boots and tried to squeeze excess water from her slacks. 'One day when we tell our grand-children about this they will never believe us. How much further?'

'All up-hill from here.'

Luckily the two friends were never down for long and soon began to see the funny side of their escapade. Two women and a pig wearing an old man's belt around her neck to which was attached two pieces of rope. One lady with a bag of fruit and vegetables to entice the sow and the other dripping wet and as she walked her boots squelched from her dip in the brook.

They left behind the leafy lane and following the mountain path were soon out on the open hillside; it was a clear, moonlit night and Edna could easily see her brother's farm.

'How much further?' asked Mildred.

'Just down there,' Edna pointed to her brother's farm.

'Good thing the night is warm I will soon dry out. You should take that bright red jumper off; if a bomber flies over you will easily be spotted as there isn't anywhere to hide up here.'

'I would be more visible without my jumper and more enticing. Anyhow, no-one has sighted bombers over this area.'

Mildred stood with her back against the open range trying to dry out her wet rear and although it was a summer night the two were glad of a hot cup of cocoa.

Harry had taken Bertha into her new home in an old pig sty. 'Haven't put her in with the young boar as they will have to get to know each other.'

'Will he know what to do?' asked Mildred.

'You are sex mad;' said Edna as they settled in two easy chairs one each side of the range until morning.

'It is only me;' called Mildred as she opened the back door into Edna's kitchen.

'Think we need something stronger than tea,' laughed Mildred. 'My father and grand-father are in a real tizzy can't repeat their language as they blamed each other. They can't report it; Grand-father has searched the village and father has been out looking for tracks. Good thing I re-locked the woodland gate before we set off and I managed this morning to put the key back so they have no idea how Bertha was stolen. We saved Bertha from the chop I can just see her rolling in the hay with her lover.'

'Now who is being the romantic; even if you roll in the hay I am sure pigs don't but here's to Bertha and all her little piglets. One little pig that didn't go to market.'

'Getting in the last word Mildred said; 'Not so 'little'.'

The End

Val Baker Addicott

Like a Phoenix Rising from the Ashes

How many times have you heard this question being asked; 'If your house was on fire what is the first thing you would grab?'

Fire; flood which is the worse? I cannot say what the feelings are of anyone who has lost their home and possessions by flood but I am in a position to voice my opinion about the heart felt loss and devastation caused by a fire and the long term effects it has on one. Here is my story.

Christmas 2005 was over; it had been a happy family time especially for my husband who delighted in spoiling our beautiful great-grand-daughter Amelia Mae. Christmas tree and decorations had been put up early so as soon as the New Year had been welcomed in I was ready to take the tree down but had been persuaded to leave it a bit longer just for Amelia.

2nd of January 2006 Emlyn knew that nothing would be open in town but it was just his routine that he would say; 'I'll just go down to see if there is anything open.'

I was tempted to start taking the decorations off the tree so unplugged it in readiness but decided to leave it for another day. Closing the sitting room door as I knew full well that our Labrador Leo, being an opportunist, would find his way onto the settee. My husband soon returned saying that there was nothing open and that he hadn't even had a cup of coffee. His next remark was; 'what's for lunch?' I was looking to see what was in the fridge when our grand-son-in-law called to drop off a cane peacock chair that they no longer wanted and I had agreed to have as my bears would look good sitting in it. 'Can't stop,' he said 'Amelia is sleeping'. I told him to leave it by the sitting room door as we were just about to have lunch.

Memories fade; or does one wipe the horrible ones from one's mind? What I can remember is seeing Leo the Lab racing up the hall his back legs almost touching his front ones. What had he done to cause him to panic? Had he knocked the chair over that Chris had just brought? The chair was where it had been placed so what had upset Leo had he heard something? I then saw smoke seeping through the closed door; I just opened it a fraction and saw lights flashing along the ceiling and smoke everywhere. I quickly closed the door and went into the front bedroom to phone the fire brigade but already the phone was dead. I called to my husband that the house was on fire and I was going to my neighbour to get help. There was no reply; I found out later that Val and Malcolm, as it was such a lovely day, had decided to go out as they hadn't had a chance over Christmas. I ran around to my neighbour on the other side and luckily they were at home and phoned for the fire brigade. Within ten minutes two fire engines arrived I saw my husband was safe and asked him where was Leo? He told me that Leo had got out with him through the patio door but with great difficulty as the door was difficult to open. I went out the back garden and called to him but Leo didn't respond; he was nowhere to be seen. Now, looking back, I wonder what made me do such a stupid thing I went back through the patio doors and I could hear a noise. My neighbour was begging me to come out as it was too dangerous; obviously the noise I could hear was the fire raging through the house. Andrew persuaded me to go with him back into his home. I kept saying; 'I want my dog; where's Leo?'

It took the two fire crews from Haverfordwest and one from Milford Haven almost an hour to extinguish the blaze; We lost irreplaceable books, antiques, records and my paintings.

I calmed down a little when a fireman came to tell me that they had found Leo hiding under one of the large shrubs in my garden. I learnt later that Labradors are very sensitive and if something goes wrong they think they are to blame. I was comforted to know Leo was safe but then seeing a police officer in the room I started to cry; 'I want my son; tell my son.'

She told me that she had already contacted Phillip at his police station and he was on his way but being over a hundred miles it would take him a couple of hours.

I was told that in less than ten minutes the fire had raged through the bungalow. I just thanked God that my husband, myself and Leo were safe. As I had had heart surgery and was on warfarin I was taken to hospital for a check-up but Emlyn had said that he was okay. My daughter was so distressed on hearing the news that she couldn't come to the hospital so sent her husband Filippo to check that I was okay. It was only when he tried explain to me how bad it really was that it really hit me. As reality set in so I began to get more and more stressed. My grand-daughter came and told me that they had only just got as far as the town when they heard the fire engines and could see smoke but little did they guess that it was our home. Reality was setting in.

Perhaps I am not stating the facts in the right context as so many things seemed to happen at the same time; my son's arrival; the loss adjuster. Luckily, if one can use that word, Emlyn had been in the insurance business for many a year. Filippo arranged for his friend Giovanni to board up the property. Word spread fast and soon there were people coming to view the tragedy; we hit the headlines in the local press having our photo taken with Leo and Amelia.

Leo had saved our lives as if we hadn't seen him running up the hall I don't know what the outcome would have been as the fire spared nothing. Almost fifty years of our life together gone up in flames. The force of the inferno could be seen by the fact that it blew out the sitting room window. How distressing it was to see bits of loved possessions thrown by the firemen onto the front garden; pages of some of the 700 books that filled the oak bookcases; pieces of my favourite pieces of china; a leg from an antique carved chair. How does one take it all in; perhaps a friend's words were a comfort; 'you had pleasure from owning it but now it is gone and you must put it from your mind.'

How much energy does it take to be strong? We had been told we could book into a hotel but Leo would have to go to kennels. No way was I putting Leo in kennels so until we could find a property to rent my daughter and son-in-law gave up their bed so that we could rest in comfort. She had the single bed in the spare room and Fil slept on the lounge floor and Leo in the kitchen. How often had I heard the saying that 'things' are often worse at night? I suppose, now looking back, I must have been hysterical. I started thinking of all that had been lost; the few possession that once belonged to my beloved grand-mother; my mother's own pastel work of Duffryn House; I began to think stupid thoughts; when I had opened the sitting room door if only I had put my hand around the corner I could have saved her painting. My grandmother's telegram on her 100th birthday from The Queen; photographs; my mind was in turmoil I was shaking with dread as reality started to set in; I couldn't stop crying Emlyn's strength was for both of us my inner strength had gone. It was only when Eryl told me that if I didn't stop crying she would call the ambulance and I would have to go to hospital; my dread of hospitals was the greater and I tried my best to stop crying.

It took a few days to find a suitable accommodation to rent as most rentals said 'no dogs'. Finally we settled in Sutton but the property was far from suitable; between the smell of oil coming from the range and the terrible state of the owner's garage abode and then to top it all rats in the garden we began looking for another property. 'It won't be for long,' my husband said when we took up residence in a dorma bungalow in the village of Hook. How wrong he was.

Leo was a happy boy he had a very large garden to play in and lovely walks in the woodland. Emlyn still went to town every morning and sometimes I went with him but all I really wanted to do was to stay in bed and hide myself away. Family and friends visited but each time the story about the fire had to be told and retold.

Now there were arguments about the choice of builder; we were in contact with a structural engineer of what was safe and what had to come down; nothing was conclusive as to the cause. One thing was clear it was not caused by our neglect as no points were overloaded. We had had alterations done before Christmas but no fault could be found.

Finally agreement was reached and Emlyn had his choice of builder; someone he had known from a lad when he had first started in the building trade. It was November before work started. The worst possible time of the year as when the roof was being put on the winds were gale force. Choosing doors; kitchen units and white goods should have been pleasurable but it was hard going as there were so many obstacles. To make things easier we chose to deal solely with Vincent Davies to replace all our furniture and curtains. Every purchase had to be put to the Insurers; every bill and every receipt.

We made Christmas special for our family as there was a new addition another great-grand-daughter Pippa Louise. Looking back I think it was the pleasure and laughter that Amelia brought to my husband that kept him going. He was my strength if only I had known then what I now know.

We went with our son and daughter-in-law to visit the warehouses where what was 'saved' had been stored; I recall very little of that visit as it was so heart-breaking; Phillip did find a picture of a rose that a friend had painted for me; a special memory that I later had re-framed and it is still hanging on my wall. Most of what was returned wasn't worth keeping. Anything of any use was given to charity and we found that the furniture smelt of smoke and even water damaged.

Come the New Year the Insurers began complaining about the money for the rental of the property a meeting was set up with the Loss Adjuster. I would never wish such a meeting on anyone. When I mentioned the cost of the new carpets the Loss Adjuster questioned it; he stated that we were running out of money. He listed expenses that had already gone out and there at the top of the list was the cost of keeping our 'saved' items in the two warehouses. My husband's advice to everyone he spoke to after the fire was always to read the small print. It was a good thing we knew our rights. After questioning our son we found that it was the Insurance Company who had suggested the storage of what had been saved. The cost was not ours.

It took a long, difficult day with the Loss Adjuster and a Quantity Surveyor to list every item that I could recall had been lost in the fire; going as far as putting a price on a tea towel. When I put a price on the teddy bears that had been destroyed I was told I could buy them cheaper on eBay; my argument was that they hadn't been bought on eBay. I lost all my art work in the fire; but again was told they weren't 'old masters' just oil on board. Finally agreement was reached but I still feel that we lost out on many items.

Then came the 'big push' the Insurance Company was insisting that we were back in the property by the end of February 2007. Two industrial heaters were installed to dry out the plaster quickly so that the property could be finished. Emlyn hadn't been satisfied with the outer wall and a metal mesh was installed before plastering. I had suggested that as the hall had been so narrow that it might be a good idea to leave the wall down making a much larger room. The fireplace and chimney breast had not been reinstated and two feet were taken off the lounge and the kitchen made bigger. Doorways and light switches now, by law, had to be suitable for anyone who might use a wheelchair. Prior to the fire my hall had had an expensive oriental wallpaper and I had plans to create a dining room with an oriental look. One good thing about Google was to search for a similar wallpaper finally I found one that had to be shipped from Germany.

The last day of February finally arrived and our return to our new home. Two furniture vans from Vincent Davies delivered our new furniture; put it together and placed exactly where I wanted. Carpets had been laid throughout the house a few days previously. Everything was at last perfect but Emlyn still felt he was in some-one else's home.

The fire was not to be the last of our distressing time. We were shopping for a television for the kitchen and a few other necessities when we heard that Phillip was looking for us. Not long after our return they arrived and by the look on their faces I guessed something was wrong and immediately assumed that it might be something had happened to one of Heidi's parents. I cannot put into words our feelings on learning that their son David, our twenty-one year old grandson had been killed in a car accident.

The months rolled by; I can now look back and see things that weren't quite right but one isn't gifted with fore-sight. Before we had left Hook Eryl had bought a BP tester and when she tried it on her dad his blood pressure was way up; his comment was that the meter was wrong. Three times she did and each time he said the same. Hot days in the summer of 2007 appeared to exhaust Emlyn. Baby Pippa had been poorly and had been hospitalized and Emlyn also had the 'flu so to protect the baby he didn't get to see a great deal of Pippa. He still adored Amelia and one Sunday when she visited with my daughter Emlyn had his photo taken with Amelia who was wearing his Stetson. The next day when he went to town he bought Amelia a cowboy hat.

Friday 20th July – Emlyn got up that morning and said he was feeling poorly and he hadn't done his insulin injection as he felt he couldn't eat anything. He decided that he wouldn't go to town his usual morning activity. As the day wore on he didn't improve but his concern was for me not for himself; by bid afternoon he said he wanted to lie down but couldn't do so as it made breathing difficult. I insisted I called the doctor and had no argument from Emlyn. Dr. Cooke phoned me and said he was stuck in a traffic jam and to get Emlyn to test his sugar level. Emlyn had no idea how to use the new tester; I had been in touch with Eryl through-out the day and with the doctor's arrival my daughter soon followed. An ambulance arrived to take Emlyn to hospital; what had happened to my tall, handsome husband? A little old man left our home. I journeyed with him and although he spoke to the paramedics he didn't appear to realize I was there.

Eryl and Filippo were waiting for me; I wanted to be with Emlyn but was told to wait with my daughter. It was the longest wait of my life. When at last we were taken to the intensive care unit and told that they had done all they could and to gather the family together it was heart-breaking. I hadn't had a chance to tell him 'I loved him' there had been no time to say 'Goodbye'. I was taken to be with him as he breathed his last breath; Eryl Lynne, Phillip and Emma all said their last 'Goodbye' as did their spouses. I thought of darling Amelia how could we tell her? For quite a while after Emlyn's death she kissed his photo, the last one that they had taken together when she wore his Stetson.

We will never know if the stress of the fire had attributed to Emlyn's demise. We had been in Pembrokeshire since 1971 but there was only one place to take Emlyn's ashes and that was back to his roots and the valley he loved; there on the hillside overlooking the River Cynon; a favourite place of mine and where we had walked with our children his ashes were spread; his spirit was free.

How can I now say that perhaps the fire was a blessing in disguise? To have gone on living surrounded by memories of almost fifty years would have been far harder for me after Emlyn's death than being in the home where everything was new and where Emlyn and I only had five months together to enjoy it.

Leo was my constant companion after Emlyn's death but in 2011 he too went to doggie heaven.

Am I the Phoenix that rose from the ashes?

The End

About the Author

Val Baker was born in Somerset just before the outbreak of WW2. When the war escalated her mother took her to live with her maternal grand-mother in the South Wales town of Mountain Ash.

Her grand-mother was her 'mother figure' as her mother died when Valerie was nine year old. Also in the family home was her grand-mother's bachelor brother Edwin who was a much loved 'father figure' as her father and mother had been estranged.

Valerie married Emlyn Addicott in 1959 and together they raised their two children Phillip and Eryl Lynne.

In 1971 the family moved to Haverfordwest in Pembrokeshire also still part of the family was grand-mother who reached her century in 1986.

Val Baker Addicott's books available from her or from Amazon:

Two novels on the drawing board for 2016.

'Ten of the Best'

'We'll Meet Again'

Val Baker
Addicott

·Baker's Dozen·

'A Stranger in Paradise'
Val Baker Addicott

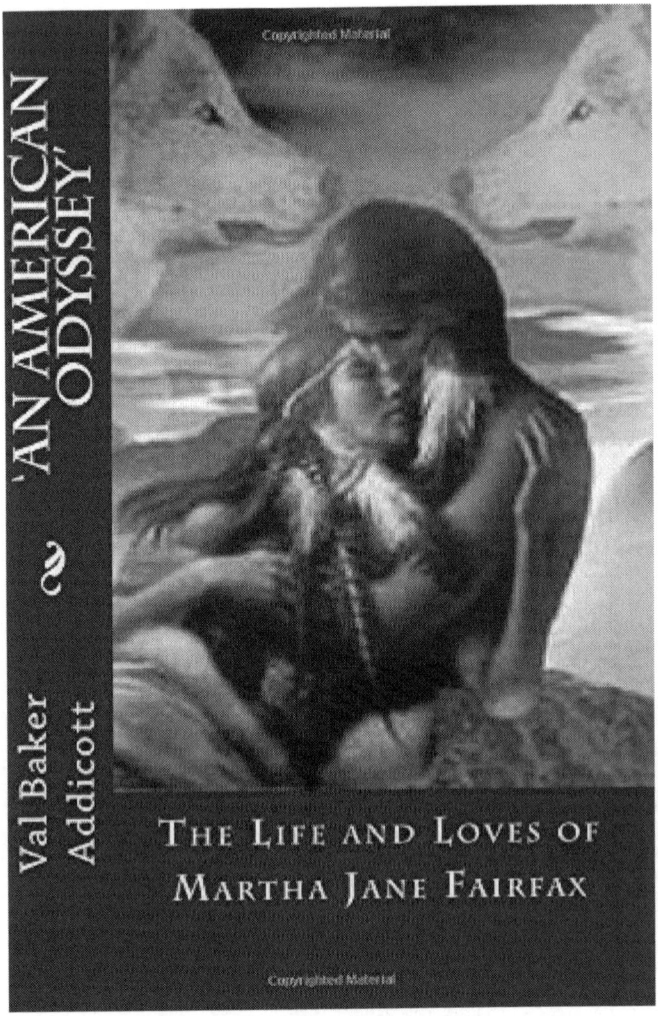
Copyrighted Material
'AN AMERICAN ODYSSEY'
Val Baker Addicott
THE LIFE AND LOVES OF
MARTHA JANE FAIRFAX
Copyrighted Material

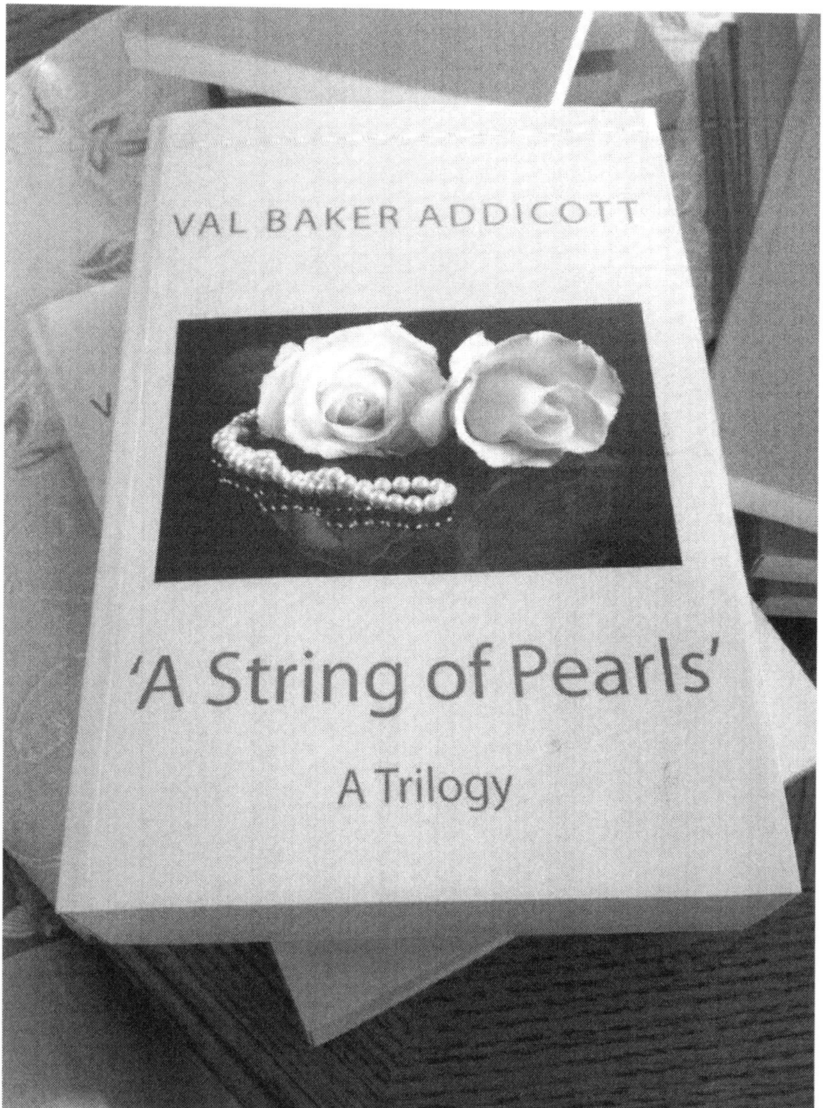
VAL BAKER ADDICOTT
'A String of Pearls'
A Trilogy

'Gwenllian
- Her Story'
'I Remember it Well'

Val Baker Addicott

'Ten of the Best'

*Stories, Recipes, Remedies,
Poetry & Sayings*

A delightful little book of short stories for one's leisure hour; poems that once learnt should never be forgotten; sayings for every occasion; grandmother's recipes and remedies. Please note that grandmother must have used these recipes and remedies but I have not tested them. A favourite with the family is grandmother's 'Puzzle Pudding'; a recipe that she kept secret until her latter years. You might also like to read her life story - 'Gwenllian - Her Story 1886-1986 - Available on Amazon.

Mammy Val's Little Book of All-Sorts

Val Baker Addicott

Baker's Dozen For Children plus St. George and the Dragon

MYTHS AND LEGENDS

VAL BAKER ADDICOTT

'Ten of the Best'

Val Baker Addicott

Happy Reading

Val Baker Addicott 2015

Made in the USA
Charleston, SC
15 October 2015